"I'm out of my element here," Blount said, shaking his head. "You Yankees live in a difficult place, yet you all seem so capable. It makes me feel as though I can't do the simplest thing. Our darkies do everything for us. You see, they—"

"Look over there," Emily interrupted. Her heart had lurched at the word "darkies." "That's Peach's Point. Now, how's that for a queer little place?"

"I've upset you, haven't I?" Blount asked. "I'm sorry, what did I say?"

"I want to remind you that Lucy is my sister, even if she isn't related by flesh and blood," Emily said. "I would be very glad if you didn't discuss your slaves when you're with me."

Blount nodded gravely. "I won't, then, if you ask me not to."

"I do," Emily said, glad of his willing acceptance. "It's a necessary condition of sailing in this boat."

"That's fine, Miss MacKenzie. I admire your loyalty. I admire you."

Flattered, Emily smiled back at him. "Oh, thank you," she murmured self-consciously. She took the tiller and steered for the harbor, blushing with confusion.

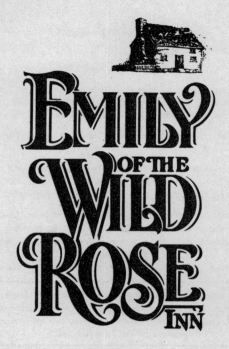

# EMILY OF THE WILD ROSE INN

### JENNIFER ARMSTRONG

BANTAM BOOKS

*New York • Toronto • London • Sydney • Auckland*

RL 5.0, age 012 and up

EMILY OF THE WILD ROSE INN

A Bantam Book/April 1994

The Starfire logo is a registered trademark of Bantam Books,
a division of Bantam Doubleday Dell Publishing Group, Inc.
Registered in U.S. Patent and Trademark Office and elsewhere.

Wild Rose Inn™ is a trademark of Daniel Weiss Associates, Inc.

ISBN 0-553-29909-3

*Published simultaneously in the United States and Canada*

*Bantam Books are published by Bantam Books, a division of Bantam Doubleday
Dell Publishing Group, Inc. Its trademark, consisting of the words "Bantam
Books" and the portrayal of a rooster, is Registered in U.S. Patent and Trademark
Office and in other countries. Marca Registrada. Bantam Books, 1540 Broadway,
New York, New York 10036.*

PRINTED IN THE UNITED STATES OF AMERICA

OPM      0 9 8 7 6 5 4 3 2 1

# EMILY OF THE WILD ROSE INN

# Chapter One

"THERE'S PLENTY OF time," Emily MacKenzie said, hopping down into her sailboat. "You know you want to go out as much as I do, Lucy."

"That's what you think," Lucy Sykes answered. The slim black girl on the dock shaded her eyes with one hand, then shook her head and laughed.

Emily looked back over her shoulder at Lucy, her adopted sister. "Don't you *want* to spend the afternoon together?" she asked. "Here we've got a whole stretch of time with not a lick of work to—"

"Yes, all right, Em," Lucy broke in. She climbed down into the *Rosy* and untied the bowline.

Emily smiled, blowing a wisp of curly brown hair from her eyes. "I knew you would say yes. I know you like I know the ABC's."

"Then I guess you hardly know me at all." Lucy snorted. "Your taste in literature has gone from bad to

1

worse. Why, I haven't seen you read anything but the *Police Gazette* since we got out of school last month."

"Well, it's a long ways more thrilling than anything we read in class," Emily said. "And what's more, I've seen you reading it, too."

"I may have glanced at it." Lucy looked over and met Emily's eyes, and both girls grinned.

They had been constant companions since the age of three, when Lucy's mother and father died in the scarlatina epidemic that had also killed Emily's mother. At sixteen, the girls worked at the Wild Rose Inn, the Mac-Kenzies' tavern and hotel. Emily still wangled as many afternoons as she could to sail in Marblehead Harbor, and as often as she could persuade Lucy, she dragged her beloved friend with her.

What might come at the end of the summer, when the yachting crowds thinned and the boats were put away and the town returned to its regular quiet pace, Emily hadn't speculated. For her, it was enough to relish each summer day and leave the future where it was, out of reach and out of mind.

Smiling, Emily turned her face to catch the breeze. The wind was fresh and salty, the taste of the rolling Atlantic in the air. In her mind she reviewed the coastal charts she knew by heart, and judged which course to take. She could hardly wait to get the *Rosy* under way.

"Oh, Emily," called a mocking voice. "Won't you teach me to sail?"

Emily stiffened.

"Micah Handy is calling you," Lucy said.

"I know that. You just ignore him," Emily whispered.

She began hauling up the mainsail. The rope was bristly across her hands, her skin was hot, and she could feel the sun breathing fire on her neck.

"Oh, Emmmm-ily!"

With a fierce scowl Emily turned around, yanking at her skirts when they snagged on a splinter. Micah Handy stood on the dock, smiling as he handed two well-dressed girls into his own trim sailboat. The girls exchanged a look as they settled themselves, and then giggled. Emily knew who they were but didn't care for them. The girls were sporting parasols, which Emily thought too ridiculous for words.

"Just you watch," she muttered to Lucy. "Those frippery things will blow inside out in no time. Yes, Micah?" she continued with elaborate politeness.

He hooked his thumbs into his vest pockets. Emily was certain that simply because the Handys' Ship hotel catered to a more elegant set than the MacKenzies' old-fashioned Wild Rose, Micah acted as lordly as a Boston millionaire. And to her great irritation, all of Marblehead had granted him the right to act the swell, as though he had earned it with his handsome profile and flashing eyes.

"Hello, Lucy. I don't see you getting out much these days," Micah called. He grinned back at Emily. "I was hoping you might give me a few pointers on how to sail in this wind."

Emily fluttered her lashes. "I'm sure as long as you

have Celia and Madeleine to help you blow all that hot air into your canvas, you'll be in fine shape."

She winked at Lucy. "That should show him," she said, and began to haul in the mainsheet.

"Lucy, I caution you to come with us," Micah warned. "After all, you know Emily like no one else. You know you can't trust her!"

"*Oh!*" Emily stifled a curse.

Lucy smiled. "I'll risk it, Micah. If I have to, I'll throw her overboard and take the tiller."

"Don't you go turning against me!" Emily wailed. "Does no one have a particle of confidence in me?"

Lucy tried to keep a straight face. "No, Em. I'm sorry."

"Lucy, get out while you can," Micah said.

"Don't you listen to him," Emily muttered, and pulled in the mainsheet. The *Rosy* leaped forward, eager as a pony. As she hauled in the sail, Emily pushed the tiller away. The *Rosy* heeled sharply as it curved through the water, and when Emily tightened the sail on their new tack, the sailboat righted itself and raced across the harbor. The sunlight streaked along beside them, speeding along the water. Emily wiped a drop of salt spray from her cheek and laughed out loud.

"Nice tack," Lucy called over the breeze.

Emily laughed again, and threw a defiant look back at the dock. Micah had his boat under sail already, and was headed toward the larger Marblehead Harbor.

"He's taking them out there to show off, just you

watch," Emily said. "He's going to point to every yacht and behave as though he owns them all."

"He's following us," Lucy told her.

Looking back, Emily saw Micah's sailboat against the bright June glare. It was heeled hard over, and the girlish screams of Micah's passengers leaped before the boat. The wind tossed one lace parasol overboard to bob like a fanciful buoy in the harbor. Emily and Lucy both shrieked with glee.

"That's the way," Emily cheered, pulling her sail closer to the wind. The *Rosy* raced toward the rocky shoreline. Above the keening of kittiwakes, she could hear Micah shouting taunts as the other boat followed.

"Come 'round on a beam reach!" Lucy said, leaning forward eagerly as the boat sped for the rocks.

Emily let go her line and shoved the tiller over. But Micah steered his boat across her wind. The *Rosy* stopped in the water, its sail flapping.

"Oh, I beg your pardon, Emily," Micah called out across the waves. He was grinning as he tacked expertly around to mock her again. "Did I do that? If only I'd had a teacher as good as you, I wouldn't have done such a crack-brain thing!"

His companions laughed, and Emily stood up in the becalmed boat. "Just you wait, Micah!" she yelled, waving her fist at him. "I'm a better sailor than you any day of the wee-*eeee*—!"

Her sentence ended in a shriek as the boom swung around and knocked her overboard. Cold water closed

5

over her head before she kicked hard and came up spitting brine. Lucy leaned her elbows on the gunwales.

"Throw me a line, Lucy," Emily gasped. Her dress dragged at her as she treaded water. Over her shoulder, she saw Micah sailing out of the harbor, the sun gleaming on his hair. The two girls smirked back at her.

"Emily," Lucy said, handing her the end of a rope. "Haven't I heard you say a smart sailor never stands up in a boat?"

"I never said that," Emily said. She reached for the gunwale.

"Oh, is that right? It must have been some other expert sailor who said that, then."

Emily let out a sorry sigh. "Well you can quit making a fool of me any time you like, Lucy. I almost drowned, and you don't seem the least bit alarmed."

"I recover fast," Lucy replied airily.

"I can see that. Now, go sit on the gun'l across from me while I climb in."

Awkwardly, Emily dragged herself over the side and plumped into the bottom of the boat. Water streamed from her, puddling in the bilges.

"You look a bit wet," Lucy observed.

Emily burst out laughing. "That I am, Lucy," she chuckled. "I am most certainly dampish." She took the pins from her wet hair and untangled her curls. The sun was already making her gingham dress steam. "Now, shall we go chase Micah all the way to Cape Cod?"

"Chase Micah Handy?" Lucy asked, her brown eyes wide. "Anybody would think you're sweet on him."

"Oh, you know that's the most ridiculous thing I ever heard," Emily retorted.

"The way you two fight, it's an easy assumption to make."

Emily squinted at her sister and wiped a drop of saltwater from her cheek. "You had a fight with Mr. Penworthy when he kicked his dog, but I never said anything about you and him being sweet on each other."

Lucy let out a peal of laughter. "That bald-headed old cuss!"

"Old cuss is right," Emily said. She grinned as she wrung out her hair. "Do you know—sometimes I believe we'll both end up marrying old cusses, as that's the only type of man that comes to the Wild Rose."

"Not me," Lucy said smilingly.

"I know, I know. You aim to marry a hero," Emily said with a show of disgust. "I notice you don't give a second look to any of the boys in town. And I'll tell you what," she went on, pointing a finger. "That's what you get from reading those novels you're so fond of. You are temperamentally unsuited to falling in love unless it's a highly romantic situation."

"I guess you think I should read less and sail more."

"Maybe," Emily said. "That's my aim."

"Then you *should* marry one of those old salts," Lucy replied with a giggle. "Pay close attention tonight and take your pick."

Emily shuddered. "Lord protect me. Every night, the same men having the same old foolish conversation. At

7

least I think it's the same conversation. I hardly listen any longer."

"They aren't talking foolishness, Emily." Lucy's smiled faded. "Abolition is a serious business, and you know full well I'm just lucky I was born to free parents."

"Oh, I know it, I know it," Emily said uncomfortably. "Now, let's get after Micah."

Lucy took the tiller and glanced back at the harbor. "Emily, the flag."

"What?" Emily looked toward the docks, crestfallen. Even from their distance, she could clearly see a red cloth waving from the top window of the Wild Rose Inn. Promising to obey the signal was the one way Emily could convince her father and older sister to let her offshore.

"Perhaps we won't see that for a few minutes," Emily said, giving her friend a hopeful look.

Lucy shook her head, and Emily sighed. As Lucy trimmed the sails, Emily cast one last look at Micah's fast-receding boat.

"I'll show him who's the better sailor," she muttered. She pushed the tiller hard around, frowning in concentration as the *Rosy* cut a tight half circle and headed for the docks. "I'll teach the unlikeliest person in all Marblehead to sail, just see if I don't."

"If you'd apply the same concentration to everything else that you apply to sailing, you'd be brilliant and make a fortune," Lucy broke in. "And you might get your chores done without me always having to remind you."

"That's a fine backhanded compliment. It so happens I prefer to preserve my powerful intellect for the exclusive

8

pursuit of the nautical arts. I gladly leave all other intellectual channels free and open to you."

Lucy clapped one hand over her eyes and shook her head. "Give me strength, Lord."

The girls brought the boat in to harbor, and as Lucy jumped to the dock, Emily threw her the bowline. Lucy made fast the boat while Emily began taking down her sail. Then Lucy bent down, and stretched out her hand to Emily.

"Now, let's get going," Lucy said. "I expect Lavinia put out the flag because there's some new guests at the Rose. Lord knows we can use the business, but she's likely to be in a terrible flurry."

"When is Lavinia not in a terrible flurry?" Emily asked, linking arms with her sister. They walked quickly through the fish-smelling boatyard and turned up an alley. "I'll tell you, she never should have married Zachary. Whaling men go whaling, so if he's not here when there's a baby coming, she shouldn't be so surprised and dismayed. I told her to marry Dr. Pennoyer, but then he went out to the Nebraska territory and for all I know has gotten himself scalped by now, so I reckon she wouldn't be any better off listening to me." She gulped for breath.

Lucy put one hand on Emily's shoulder and solemnly shook her head. "Nobody would ever take your advice, Emily, don't worry about that."

"Well, I never heard such a—"

"Hey, gal, turn around there," called a rough voice from behind them.

Gaping with astonishment, Emily looked over her

9

shoulder. A squint-eyed man with side whiskers and a soiled coat was hurrying after them from the boatyard. He took Lucy's arm and swung her sharply around to face him.

"Let me get a good look at you," he said.

"Let me go!" Lucy struggled to pull her arm away.

"I beg your pardon, mister!" Emily burst out. "What do you mean by accosting us in the street?"

He gave her a sour look. "This nigger looks like a runaway I'm after, a gal from Maryland. There's a gang of abolitionist outlaws around here somewheres smuggling the legal property of honest folk down South, and I aim to find them out."

Emily put her arms around Lucy and looked at the man with loathing. "A bounty hunter, how low," she muttered.

"I am not a slave." Lucy's breathing was harsh and loud. "My parents were born free."

"Oh, I'm to believe you, am I?" The bounty hunter cleared his throat and spat into the street. "I like that."

Emily glared at him. "Lucy is no slave, as anyone could tell just by looking at her. We've had bounty hunters in Marblehead before, and I'll tell you, you won't be making many friends. Let us pass and leave us be. Come on, Lucy."

With her arm supporting a shaking Lucy, she turned and marched up the street. "What a low, mean occupation," Emily said. "And did you see his coat? It looked just as though he'd been scrubbing potatoes with it. He stank, too."

Emily stopped and looked behind her. The bounty hunter was watching them. She gave him the coldest stare she was capable of, and then turned her back on him, sure she had disposed of that problem with perfect finality.

# Chapter Two

"Now, LET'S HURRY up," Emily said, letting go of Lucy's arm.

But Lucy hung back. There was a faint line of sweat on her upper lip, and she wiped it off with one quick movement. Her throat worked in a dry swallow.

"Oh, Lucy," Emily said, giving her friend a fierce hug. "Don't upset yourself over him. Those bounty hunters come sniffing around, but while any MacKenzie has breath, you're safe."

"I know I'm safe," Lucy faltered.

"And there's not one single Negro in Marblehead that can't prove he ain't a slave," Emily continued.

"Emily, you don't—" With a frown, Lucy glanced back over her shoulder, and then shook her head.

"I wonder what he meant about a local gang of outlaws?" Emily said with a gleam in her eyes. "Who could that be in Marblehead? Imagine taking such risks for strangers."

"I can imagine it," Lucy said softly.

"Well, if your imagination is that good, I wish you'd help me think of some diabolical way to work my revenge on Micah," Emily said, kicking a clamshell that went skittering through the dust. "I'm soaking wet, and I want to go home." She stepped out onto Front Street. "Come on." Emily reached back and tugged Lucy's arm.

Hand in hand, they walked down the busy street that echoed the line of the shore. Houses stood shoulder to shoulder on either side, brass knockers polished, windows glinting in the summer sun. Month by month, whalers and merchants were throwing up new houses, packing additions onto old ones, importing grand furnishings from France and England and the Orient until japanned desks and ormolu clocks were fairly spilling through the windows. Marblehead was bursting at the seams.

And because the old part of town was crammed to capacity, new ground was being broken for homes elaborate enough for the newly rich. Through alleys and passageways, glimpses of Marblehead Neck across the harbor showed the opulent vacation homes sprouting up like fairy castles while in the harbor itself, dowdy old fishing craft lumbered beside sleek clippers and elegant racing yachts.

As Emily and Lucy crossed a narrow alley, a carriage trundled through, almost scraping the buildings on either side. The girls waited while the driver made the turn, and then followed it, sidestepping a pile of horse droppings. At the garden gate, Emily struggled with the latch that always stuck, catching the heavy scent of the red roses twining along the fence. The gate swung open and they both hurried into the sprawling house.

"Lavinia!" Emily called, opening first one door and then another. The old hostelry smelled of woodsmoke and whale oil, and the scarred plank floors echoed with two hundred years of fishermen's feet. In the low-ceilinged taproom at the front of the house, a few men sat playing checkers and sipping beer. Emily's father waved a greeting from the bar.

Emily hurried down the hallway, nearly tripping over a worn oilcloth runner. "Lavinia? We're here! We were just about set to sail to an exotic port, but Lucy saw your flag. Lavinia?"

The door to the best parlor opened and Lavinia Mill, eight months pregnant, poked her head out into the corridor. Her face was pink with embarrassment. "Hush, Emily!" she whispered. "You're shouting like a sailor."

"Well, I'm sorry, I was looking for you," Emily said as Lucy joined them in the doorway. Emily tried to peek past her sister into the parlor. "Who's in there? The queen of England?" She stepped inside.

Still blushing, Lavinia backed away. "Mr. and Mrs. Stockwell, my sister, Emily MacKenzie," she said with all the dignity she could summon. "And our adopted sister, Lucy Sykes."

Emily and Lucy both halted on the threshold. Before them, in the homey inn's best room, was a tableau straight from the pages of the latest lady's magazine. A pale woman in lace bonnet and fichu sat fanning herself

14

on an armchair; beside her, a handsome young man in a well-cut suit leaned over her, offering a glass of lemon-water; and at the window, a fierce-looking man in traveling clothes held the *Marblehead Gazette* at arm's length, scowling with bad temper. All three of them widened their eyes at Emily's bedraggled appearance.

"How do you do?" Emily said with a smile. "I apologize for the condition of my clothes, but I was beset in the harbor by a rascal."

The woman raised a tiny handkerchief to her mouth. "Mercy."

"Don't mind her," Lucy suggested. "She's just embarrassed that she fell out of her own boat. Lavinia and I are pretty civilized, though, and we'll see that you're comfortable."

"Yes, you will," Mr. Stockwell said curtly.

Lucy blinked at his unexpected rudeness, and Emily put her arm protectively around her waist.

"Don't pay any attention to Emily's tales," Lavinia said quickly. "She may look like a savage, Mrs. Stockwell, but she's a good kind girl and will be perfectly happy to make your visit with us a comfortable one," she added, sending a meaningful look in Emily's direction.

"Oh, I'm in raptures," Emily replied. She was irked at Mr. Stockwell's manner and surprised at the pains Lavinia was taking to placate them. "I'm fairly transported with joy."

The young man beside Mrs. Stockwell met Emily's eyes and he sent her a slow, knowing smile.

"The Stockwells are visiting Marblehead for the first

time," Lavinia went on in a pointedly cheerful voice. "They've traveled all the way from Richmond, Virginia, girls. And we're *delighted* they chose to stay here at the Wild Rose."

"I expect you didn't choose us on anyone's personal recommendation, then," Emily said. "The town must be full up. I don't expect you run into many sailors and itinerant tradesmen where you live. But we make all guests feel welcome."

"Emily!" Lavinia laughed. "She is such a humorist, Mr. and Mrs. Stockwell."

"Indeed, there weren't any rooms available at the other establishments," Mrs. Stockwell said, looking anxiously at her husband.

"Ordinarily we would choose a more convenient hotel," Mr. Stockwell said. "All the more reason I expect you'll make suitable arrangements for our comfort."

"We'll do our best, sir," Lucy said.

Mr. Stockwell gave her a blank look and then turned deliberately away. Emily heard the quick intake of Lucy's breath before Lucy backed out of the room.

"I'll just go get all our gold and silver to lay around," Emily announced loudly. "I hope that'll make you feel at home."

"Mr. Stockwell," Lavinia said, wringing her hands together, "I do beg your pardon for Emily's sake. Our mother died when she was a mere child, and our father and I have been managing the place on our own, and my husband—he's first mate on the whaler *Betty Lynn,* you know, has not been home in months, they're in the Sand-

16

wich Islands, I think—my sister inherited her high temper from our mother. I'm afraid she's been apt to run somewhat wild but ever so interesting," she said in a rambling way.

Lavinia pressed one hand to her flushed cheek and let out a sigh. Then she turned to Emily with such a pleading look in her eyes that Emily's heart melted and she repented of her sass. Emily put one arm around her sister's shoulder and propelled her out into the corridor.

"I'm sorry I'm acting like a heathen, but I don't know why you act as though they're royalty. Maybe they should go to a more refined establishment if we have to treat them like porcelain dolls. And I don't like the way they stare at Lucy like she's a sea monster. Did you notice that?"

"They'll find the Wild Rose Inn suits them just fine, and we'll just ignore their manners or lack of. Maybe you'd like to see that their rooms have the best linen. And move mother's mirror into Mrs. Stockwell's room. We do indeed want them as our guests. We need their business."

Emily bit back another tart reply as Lavinia returned to the parlor. Lucy came slowly around the corner of the hallway, stopping when she saw Emily.

"Come on," Emily whispered. "We'd best put on our Sunday clothes and remember to say yes ma'am and no sir, or else Lavinia will have an attack of the vapors and the baby'll come early and then we'll be in quite a box."

"I happen to agree with you this time. I wish those folks wouldn't stay here," Lucy said in a strained voice.

Emily nodded before leading the way down the corridor. "For once I wish our trade would go over to the Ship. Let the high-handed Handys contend with those Stockwells. I'm sorry they were mean to you," she added.

She stopped under a knicked harpoon mounted on the corridor wall. "Do you know, Lavvy wants Mother's mirror in that lady's room? Now, I ask you, does that seem right?"

"No," Lucy replied. She shook her head and looked back down the corridor. "It does not seem right at all. There is more and more that does not seem right to me."

"Nor do I want to tolerate their rude behavior," Emily went on hotly. She was putting her shoulder to a door hidden in the paneling when Lucy clutched her arm. "Wait!"

But Emily had pushed open the door before Lucy's objection registered. Then she halted.

"Yes? What is it?"

Lucy glanced inside and then away. "Oh, I thought I'd forgotten something. Never mind me."

Emily shrugged and then led the way through a dark, cramped passage built between the walls. After years of adding on at the Wild Rose, the place was a hodgepodge of rooms, stairs, and passages. Emily and Lucy knew the shortest routes from one end of the rambling house to the other, and not every passageway was apparent to the occasional guest. Hiding games had been the girls' favorite pastime as children, and on occasion, Emily was still tempted to slip out of sight when there were too many chores for her liking.

"Do you remember?" Emily mused as she and Lucy

went through the narrow passage. "That time when we tried to go through here and found both ends locked? I was as mad as a hornet."

Lucy didn't reply, being too busy holding back her sneezes as their feet raised dust in the stuffy space.

"And then I tried prying it open with a poker and didn't Father cut up a fuss!" Emily went on with a laugh. She shouldered open the door at the opposite end. "You'd think he was Great-grandpa John hiding smuggled rum from the British."

"Uncle Marcus never scolded unless we needed it," Lucy said. She followed Emily out into another corridor and began to mount the staircase. "I expect he had a reason to get so mad."

Emily climbed behind her friend. "Well, I don't know what that reason could have been. I swore I'd run away to sea if he punished me one more time. I wanted to get on a clipper ship and go to California with the gold miners."

Smiling at the memory, Emily led the way up to another set of stairs leading to a third-story attic. Daylight filtered in from the windows at either end, illuminating a jumble of discarded furniture: gouged benches, narrow bedsteads, and rickety chairs, a three-legged table in need of mending, lamps with cracked glass globes, even two or three aged barrels. Fashions had come and gone in America, prompting the MacKenzie family to consign old things to the attic and buy new, but nothing had been thrown away.

As Emily threaded her way through the clutter, Lucy

went to one of the windows and stood looking out at the roofs and widow's walks of Marblehead.

"Where are those best linen sheets?—phew! Look at the dust!" Emily exclaimed.

She brushed her sleeve across the top of a brass-studded sea chest and tipped back the lid. The scent of lavender and lemon balm rose up into her face, and a muslin sachet fell from the folds of a delicately embroidered sheet as Emily picked it up.

"Look at this," she said quietly. "My mother stitched these." Emily smoothed the sheet with her hand and traced the dainty floral pattern with the tip of one finger. "Oh, sometimes I just feel so low, don't you?" she added with a sigh.

Lucy did not answer. Emily frowned as she regarded her sister's stiff back. "What is it?" she asked. "You've hardly said a word in the last five minutes."

Very slowly, Lucy turned around. Her face was thrown into deep shadow as the light from the window made a nimbus about her head. Emily could not see Lucy's expression.

"Those Stockwells," Lucy said. "They brought a slave with them."

"What?" Emily dropped the sheet into the chest and sat back on her heels.

"A young fellow."

"My gracious. Where is he now?"

Lucy turned her head, and the light slanted across her cheekbone. "In the kitchen."

"My gracious," Emily repeated faintly. She blew a

wisp of hair from her forehead. "I suppose we can find room for him. I wonder if Lavinia knows. I wonder if she knew about him before she quoted a rate for room and board."

Lucy glanced at Emily. "I'll see if Lavinia wants me," she murmured, and then hurried down the stairs.

Emily listened to Lucy's footsteps fade out of earshot. Then she snatched up the sheets and slammed the trunk shut.

After seeing that the best guest rooms were aired and ready, Emily returned downstairs to talk to Lavinia about accommodations for the Stockwells' servant. She poked her head into the dining room, which was silent and empty in the afternoon's heat. She quickly shut the door again and made her way through the maze of passages to the taproom.

"Hello, Father," she said, ducking under the partition to join him behind the bar.

"Hello, pet," Mr. MacKenzie replied absently. He was frowning over columns of numbers in his ledger, and his fingers were stained with ink. His steel-nibbed pen scratched busily in counterpoint to the hum of men's voices from the tables by the windows. There was a click of whale-ivory checkers tapping across the checkerboards.

"Lavvy is putting on her best bib and tucker for these people from Virginia," Emily said, slipping her arm through her father's. "Do you suppose she realized they brought a slave with them?"

Marcus MacKenzie's pen stopped scratching. "They did, did they?"

"Yes," Emily said. "And I'm trying to think where we'll put him up."

"That's not your bother," her father said, giving her cheek a pat.

"Yes, but—"

"Lavvy and I will take care of everything, Emmy," Mr. MacKenzie insisted. "Now, go see what she needs."

Emily removed her arm from his. It was his way to treat her still as the poor motherless child who had cried in her sleep. But as Emily glanced at his ledger full of figures and lines and names from under her lashes, she gave a slight sigh. It was just as well. The less responsibility they gave her, the more time she had for sailing and skylarking. Adding up accounts was not her notion of an enjoyable day.

"Oh, by the way," Mr. MacKenzie added, "have you seen Lucy?"

"A few minutes ago, but I don't know where she is," Emily replied.

"Tell her to keep clear of these new guests, will you? I think it's best. They're not likely to think of her as we do." Mr. MacKenzie shut his book with a snap. "Now, Emily, I wrote out a passage from Plato's *Republic* for you to translate. How are you coming along with it?"

"Ah . . ." Emily chewed her lip for a moment, and then met her father's eyes. "I haven't begun yet, Father, but I will."

"This evening?"

"Ah . . . Yes, yes, I will," Emily agreed with a sigh.

He smiled at her. "Now then, go on back to work. Lavvy's sure to need you."

Emily ducked back under the partition and left the tavern. As she turned the corner into the corridor, the Stockwells' son stepped through the parlor door. He smiled when he saw her.

"Hello," he said, making a small bow. "Something tells me we've been shunted into the back room and that interesting things are happening if only I knew where."

"If you call a half-dozen fishermen drinking beer and playing checkers interesting, you have a different view of stimulation from what mine is," Emily said, laughing.

He returned her smile. "That girl, Lucy—Mrs. Mill called her your sister?" he asked.

"Yes," Emily said, lifting her chin. "Sister. We grew up together, and I love her dearly."

"You're very loyal," he said, his smile deepening. "Our Moses was once a playfellow of mine. But as we grew older . . ."

Emily gave him a sharp look. "Moses? Is he the servant you brought? I need to ask," she said when he nodded. "We've got a little box-room, like an attic, at the back of the second floor. Will that do for him?"

Mr. Stockwell's voice came from the parlor. "The barn will be sufficient for him," he said. He came to the door, and gave his son a reproachful look. "Bring some claret," he added sharply as he turned to reenter the parlor. "This wait is making Mrs. Stockwell unwell."

Emily gaped at the man's rudeness to his own son. Then it struck her that the man had been speaking to *her*

23

in that imperious tone, and the color drained from her face.

"Why, I never," she gasped, blinking in surprise. She rounded on the son. "I am not used to being treated as though I were—a—a—"

Instantly the young man held up both hands in surrender. "I apologize. I really do," he said. He glanced back at the parlor door and lowered his voice, leaning toward her like a conspirator. "I'm afraid you will find my family something of a handful."

Emily raised her eyebrows. "I will, will I?"

"I am very much afraid so," he repeated in the same soft voice. "My mother suffers from all sorts of complaints. And my father suffers from her complaints, too."

Emily grinned. "I thought gentlemen from Virginia were meant to act with the highest degree of dutiful love and chivalry toward their parents," she said in a scandalized whisper.

"Oh, we are, we are," he replied. "I assure you, keeping my mother and father quiet—quiet in their hearts and minds, that is—is my greatest concern." His eyes, which were dark brown, glinted with laughter.

Emily allowed herself a quick appraising glance as he turned to examine an oil painting of a pre-Revolutionary ship. He was dressed in the height of fashion, in tight buckskin breeches and a cutaway coat. With his smooth manners and easy grace, Emily lumped him in the same category as the grandees that strolled the marbled porticos of the Neck's great mansions. They came to Marblehead to be seen, to sport fanciful sailing costumes completely alien to the real sailors and fishermen of Massachusetts, to take tea with ladies and attend musical evenings.

The Stockwells' son was clearly one of these, Emily decided. It was impossible to be more *unlike* a true sailor than this young man. But underneath his outward polish there was obviously a hint of mischief, and he seemed not to share his parents' cold manner. That was certainly an improvement on the type.

"Gracious!" she exclaimed suddenly.

He turned to her politely. "Yes?"

"You don't know how to sail, do you?" Emily accused him.

"No, I have to admit, I've never even been on a sailboat," he said, "although I suggested Marblehead as our destination because I've always wanted to learn. We meant to spend the summer at Saratoga but changed our plans suddenly."

"That's first-rate. *I'll* teach you to sail," Emily told him.

"I'm delighted and honored," he replied with a beaming smile. "We certainly picked the right place to stay. But are you sure you can teach me?"

Emily grinned. She was sure she had picked the least able sailor in all of Massachusetts. But teach him to sail she would.

"I'm quite sure," she said, turning away with a cheerful bounce in her step. Then she stopped herself and looked back. "What's your name?"

"Blount," he said, his smile wider than ever. He had a dimple in his left cheek.

"And my name is Emily," she replied. "But from now on, you can call me Captain."

She heard his rich laugh follow her as she went up the stairs, and smiled to herself. "Just you wait, Micah. Just you wait."

At the top of the stairs Emily paused. She might have offered to teach Blount Stockwell sailing to prove a point to Micah Handy, but she was also pleasantly sure that she would have a delightful time doing so.

# Chapter Three

PROMPTLY AT SIX o'clock that evening the dinner bell rang in the dining room, and there was an unmannerly rush from the tavern. Besides the overnight guests, there were numerous local bachelors who took their evening meal at the Wild Rose Inn; the schoolteacher, three unmarried ministers, a widowed sea captain or two, as well as various and sundry other wifeless men who looked forward to the Wild Rose's evening meal and Lavinia's excellent cooking. Noticeably absent from the communal tables were the Stockwells, who insisted upon being served privately in the parlor.

"You see, they're too high and mighty for us," Emily said as she loaded a tray of food for them in the kitchen. "I never thought I'd see the day when I'd have to wait on someone hand and foot. It doesn't hardly seem democratic to me."

"Now, you hush," Lavinia said crossly, pushing up her sleeves. "You don't have to wait on them at all, for you know perfectly well their servant will wait at table. Just take in the tray. And no more grumbling right now."

"I wasn't grumbling," Emily replied as she backed into the door. The smells of codfish cake and brown bread and carrots rose into her face. "But we didn't fight a Revolution to treat some folks like lords and ladies."

"I didn't see you fighting any Revolution," Lucy said, coming into the kitchen from the corridor. "All you ever fight is Micah Handy."

Emily stuck her tongue out, and Lavinia laughed. "Lucy, you have an even saucier mouth than Emily," Lavinia said.

"I guess I must be a MacKenzie, after all."

"You are, dear," Lavinia assured her with a smile.

Emily bore the tray off to the parlor. Lucy's and Lavinia's voices, pitched low and murmuring, followed her.

At the parlor door she paused, drew a deep breath, and awkwardly adjusted the heavy tray onto one hand so that she could knock. The door opened and a young black man held it wide for her to enter.

"I brought dinner," Emily said unnecessarily. She eyed Moses with some curiosity, having seen few slaves. Marblehead was populated by numerous free blacks, but slaves were an uncommon sight. The Stockwells' servant was tall, and his skin was very dark against the white neck of his shirt. She gave him a smile, which he seemed not to see.

"Thank you," Mrs. Stockwell prompted from inside the room.

"Oh, yes, here it is," Emily said, hurrying in.

28

She set the tray on the sideboard and began lifting the covers off the dishes one by one. "My sister's special codfish cakes, brown bread, carrots, and I can bring beer, cider, wine, sarsaparilla, buttermilk, whatever you might like. And we have coffee on the fire or we can make tea."

"Don't stand there by the door like a post, Moses," Mr. Stockwell ordered. "You're as stupid as a mule."

"Yes, sir," Moses said quietly, moving to the sideboard.

Mrs. Stockwell sighed. "I did so wish to go to Saratoga this summer. Is there always such a smell of fish in the air in this town?" She waved her scented handkerchief in front of her face. "I was led to believe this was a yachting center."

"It is, Mother," Blount said. He grinned at Emily. "But it is still a fishing port, isn't that right, Captain?"

Emily darted him an amused glance. "Why, the banks are still full, that's certain."

"Banks?" Mrs. Stockwell repeated. She looked helplessly from her son to her husband, and Moses placed a plate of dinner in front of her. "I'm afraid I fail to see the connection."

"Fishing banks, ma'am," Emily explained. "They're up there by—"

"Thank you, Miss MacKenzie," Mr. Stockwell interrupted. He cut his food apart suspiciously with the side of his fork. "That will be all. Moses, what have you done with the butter?"

Emily swallowed the anger that rose instantly in her

throat. She stalked back to the sideboard and picked up the empty tray.

"Just give a shout if you need anything," she muttered.

Then she thumped the door shut behind her and raced down the corridor.

"Ohh!" she cried out, bursting into the kitchen. "If I were a man . . ." She trailed off in exasperation.

Lavinia turned a pan of steaming gingerbread upside down onto a plate and began cutting it into squares with a knife. "What is it now?" she asked. Her swollen body moved sluggishly in the heat of the kitchen.

"Oh, Lavvy, here, let me," Emily said, taking the knife from her sister. "You sit down and rest. You look ready to drop. It's those Stockwells, what else?" she continued.

Sighing, Lavinia lowered herself into a chair, one hand at the small of her back. Her forehead was creased with weariness and worry. "Please don't make trouble," she begged. "I wish that sometimes you might think before you speak, Emily. You never do."

"I'll try," Emily promised, leaning over to plant a swift kiss on her sister's cheek.

"Thank you. You're a dear," Lavinia said. "I don't like that man any more than you do, Em, but I'm not going to brawl with him."

Emily shrugged. "The way he speaks to that slave—Moses is what he's called—it's just the rudest treatment I ever saw. He was rude enough to me, but at least he didn't call me a stupid mule."

30

Lavinia rested her chin on her hand. "It's a scandal."

"And besides," Emily went on, seating herself again at the table. "It doesn't look right, does it? After all, the Anti-Slavery Society meets here every week. What will they say?"

"Never you mind what they'll say about it," Lavinia said. "You never pay the meetings any attention anyway."

"Yes, but what *will* they say?" Emily pressed on. She knew that they met to discuss abolition, but to her mind, slavery was a Southern problem and had little to do with the people of Massachusetts. Although the group held regular discussions at the Wild Rose, she had never paid much attention to their conversation. Her father and Lavinia held strong opinions on the subject of abolition, but Emily had never cared for sermons on morality or politics, and squirmed uncomfortably whenever the subject arose. More often than not, Mr. MacKenzie told her to run along, and she was always glad to escape to the fireplace, where the old sailors never ceased to pass around ships' tales like a bowl full of oranges.

"I guess they won't like us having a slave right here under our own roof," Emily went on.

"No, they won't much like having slave owners here," Lavinia said tiredly.

Emily looked at her sister's lowered eyes and felt a pang of remorse. She wouldn't raise troubling questions and issues if they only served to upset Lavinia. Her sister had enough to worry about.

"I'll be polite," Emily promised again. "But except for the son, you can't make me like them."

Lavinia's smile faded. "No, you can't make me like them, either. But they came to us, and we'd be fools to drive them away now."

"Why?"

Lavinia hesitated. "Because we need the business," she explained after a pause. "Now be a darling and take that gingerbread into the dining room."

By the time Emily and Lucy had finished clearing dinner, drawing and heating water, and washing the dishes, the taproom of the Wild Rose Inn was filled with the companionable hum of voices. Emily dried her wet hands and tossed the towel over the back of a chair. Awaiting her on the table was a paper covered in her father's small, neat hand, line after line of Latin marching across the page like Roman legions. Emily shuddered.

"I'm going to get some ginger beer," she announced. "Do you want any, Lucy?"

Lucy had just settled herself by the kitchen's brightest lamp with her McGuffey's reader. "No, thanks for asking," she said, her eyes on a page of soliloquies from Shakespeare.

With a shrug, Emily left the hot kitchen, pausing in the hall to flap her skirts a bit and cool off her legs. There was a gentle creaking sound, and she glanced blushingly behind her, but there was no one. The building itself kept up a rambling, lackadaisical monologue, settling and sighing as though recalling and repeating the conversations it had heard over the last two centuries.

Fanning her legs, Emily tilted her head back and listened for a moment to the voice of the house. Then she touched the wooden wainscoting for good luck and went into the taproom.

"There now, there's our girl," a tiny, hunchbacked old man cackled from the fireplace. His eyes almost disappeared in the maze of wrinkles in his leathery face.

"Good evening, Mr. Trelawney!" Emily shouted, nodding extravagantly to him and smiling wide. "HOW ARE YOU TONIGHT?"

He cupped one hand to his ear and bobbed his head in return. "Oh, first-rate, first-rate. You're growing fast, Emily. Quite a beauty for a little girl."

"I'm SIXTEEN, Mr. Trelawney!" Emily shouted to him, not for the first time. "I'm a grown-up girl, now!"

He chuckled and nodded over his beer. "That's right. That's right," he said.

With an affectionate smile, Emily left the old man and threaded her way through the crowded room, greeting familiar friends of the establishment. The light from a dozen whale-oil lamps shed a glow over the room, glinting on tables polished smooth by hundreds of hands, turning cigar smoke into misty, wreathing clouds, transforming old pewter tankards into silver beakers. The crowd was as much of a hodgepodge as the inn itself: there were white men and black, faces with hints of Indian blood, even a sailor whose distinctive features proclaimed him a Maori of the South Seas. Their voices all blended together in one loud surf of sound.

Emily's minister beckoned to her from a nearby table.

"Good evening, Mr. Polk," Emily said cheerfully. She

33

leaned close and laid one finger beside her nose. "I believe there's just the slimmest bit of gingerbread left over. Do you want it?"

Mr. Polk patted her hand. "That's a kind offer, but no, thank you." He frowned, putting furrows across the dome of his high, bald forehead. "Tell me, Emily. Is it true that there are slave owners putting up here at the Wild Rose?"

"Yes, it is true," Emily said, uncomfortably remembering his many sermons about the villainy and sin of slavery.

"That's a sorry affair for this establishment," Mr. Polk said. He took off his spectacles and polished them with a voluminous handkerchief. "God did not intend for us to enslave our brothers and sisters." Several men sitting nearby nodded in agreement at his words.

"I know it," Emily replied, nervously trying to recall pertinent verses from the Bible and wishing she had paid more attention in church. "But we at least have nothing to reproach ourselves with. Lucy is one of our own family."

"That is so," Mr. MacKenzie chimed in, bringing over a tray of brimming glasses. He set them one by one on the table in front of three merchants. "It was our Christian duty to take her in, and we have never regretted it."

"That is to your credit, MacKenzie," said Mr. Ledue from the dry-goods store. He was small and spry and excitable, and jiggled up and down with agitation as he spoke. "Nevertheless, our Christian duty and charity must extend beyond our own doorsteps."

Mr. Ingersoll, senior clerk at the Massachusetts and China Shipping Company, cleared his throat with a phlegmatic cough. "You speak of abolition," he said portentously.

"*Naturally,* I speak of abolition," Mr. Ledue cried out, nearly popping off his seat. "But more besides. Much more besides!"

As Emily collected empty glasses, she noticed her father standing in the door to the street. By craning her neck, she saw that he was speaking to the bounty hunter who had accosted Lucy in the street. Her father was shaking his head. Emily made her way closer.

"The name's Pinkham," the bounty hunter said in a bluff voice. "Phineas Pinkham, staying at Mrs. Coswell's boardinghouse."

"I'll remember that," Mr. MacKenzie said quietly. "But as I said before, Mr. Pinkham, I have no information to give you, nor would I if I had any."

Mr. Pinkham scratched his cheek with a knob-knuckled finger, trying to see over Mr. MacKenzie's shoulder. "They's an abolition meeting a-going on here tonight, is that right?"

Emily's father began to close the door. "Good night, sir. My regards to Mrs. Coswell."

With a smile, Mr. Pinkham backed away and disappeared into the darkness of the street.

"He's a bounty hunter, Father," Emily whispered. "Don't you serve him. He was horrible to Lucy."

"He won't set foot in this house," her father said. "You can rely on that."

"I wonder that Mrs. Coswell would put him up," Emily continued.

Mr. MacKenzie put one arm across her shoulders. "You forget that Mrs. Coswell is a poor widow lady, Emily. We are sometimes compelled by rude necessity to do what we wish we didn't."

"Yes, Father," Emily said, slipping away before he had the chance to expound on a moral lesson.

As Emily made her way through the crowded room, she heard Mr. Ingersoll declaim loudly over the "pernicious fomenters" of states' rights. His listeners nodded in agreement and interrupted one another with their opinions. Emily saw Blount Stockwell come in, take a seat in a corner, and open a small sketchbook on the table. She felt a thrill of curiosity as she wondered what he would make of the debate sparked by his family.

Mr. Ledue jabbed one bony finger into the air for emphasis, as though prodding Almighty God for attention. "I say the states who make their own rules and morals little reckon what harm they do to us all."

" 'If a house be divided against itself, that house cannot stand,' " the Reverend Mr. Polk quoted. "Mark, chapter three, verse twenty-five."

"That fellow Lincoln from Illinois gave the same passage at the Republican Convention just last week!" Mr. Ledue cried. "I read it in the newspaper!"

"Aye, and I do agree with him, Mr. Ledue," said a grizzled, one-armed retired whaler who was aptly named Boats. "The republic is very like a whaling ship, and President Buchanan is our captain. Each soul, or state, if you

36

will, has his own skills and chores to do, be it with the harpoon, the cutting spade, or the oar. But they all work in aid of one goal: to catch the whale and bring the parmacety to port."

"Hear, hear," Mr. Ingersoll rumbled.

"Now I ask you," Mr. Boats continued, holding out his one hand and fixing the group with a narrow stare. "If every man-jack on the ship pursues naught but his own purposes, would not that ship founder? I ask you, would it not founder?"

"It would," Mr. Polk agreed. "The harpooners need the rowers, the boilers need the cutters, and so on. And likewise it is with the states."

Mr. Ledue jabbed his finger at heaven's soles again. "Just so! Just so! These states' rights seditionists will pilot us all to shipwreck and financial devastation!"

"But what if the whaling ship goes down in foul weather?" a new voice broke in.

All heads turned to look at Blount. He tipped his head to one side and smiled. "If through no fault of the boiler or the harpooner, the ship goes down, do they not also perish with the careless pilot?"

"That is undeniably so," Mr. Boats said with narrowed eyes. "But lay your argument out so we may take a good look at it, young man."

Blount gestured with his pencil. "I only wish to point out that the republic is in fact *not* a whaling ship, that our union is made up of separate states with their own purposes and requirements. Did we fight our way free of England only to be dictated to by a homegrown tyranny? I don't see that we made such a bargain, if that is the case."

"What tyranny do you speak of?" Mr. Ingersoll demanded, his eyebrows bristling mightily. "Our President?"

"Oh, Buchanan's no good," the minister suddenly broke in. "He believes that though slavery is wrong under God's law it is not unconstitutional."

"So you believe America's laws must come after God's laws," Blount inquired.

"Absolutely not!" Mr. Ledue cried passionately. "This is not a theocracy, this is a democracy!"

"A democracy of Christian men, however—"

"Or would you have us govern without moral guidance—"

The argument swept around the tables like a whirling waterspout, drawing everyone into its vortex. Emily shook her head. Whenever two Marbleheaders got together, a political debate was sure to break out, and she'd long since made a practice of ignoring the arguments that rang out at the Wild Rose each night. They were as regular and dependable as the stars in their orbits, and concerned Emily just as little.

She poured herself some ginger beer at the bar, and when she turned around, glass in hand, Micah Handy was beside her. Emily was so startled, she jumped, ginger beer splashing onto her dress.

"Oh, look what you made me do," she wailed. "I can't imagine you're welcome anywhere if you make a habit of sneaking up on people."

Micah grinned, his gold-lashed eyes impudent as always. "I wasn't sneaking, Emily."

"Well, then, if you didn't come here for the sole purpose of provoking me, I'm sure I don't know what you're doing here."

"You think I have nothing better to do than make you slop yourself?" he asked.

Emily flushed, and wiped at the stain on her dress with a cloth. A fly settled on the spot, adding to her humiliation. "Well, then, what are you doing here?" she asked. "I'm sure you have politer company at the Ship."

"Oh, I like to look around," Micah said, giving her another cocky grin and surveying the noisy, smoky room. "Why, there's my good friend the Reverend Mr. Polk."

"I doubt he is a friend of yours," Emily muttered. "I didn't see you in church last Sunday."

Micah laughed. "Don't be too sure who my friends are, Emily. Why, I might be here to join the Anti-Slavery Society. Did you ever consider that?"

She lifted her chin. "The day you ever care about anyone but yourself will be the day I grow a curly tail." She turned around with a flounce of her dress and walked haughtily out of the room, with Micah's laughter following her every step of the way.

# Chapter Four

EMILY AWOKE THE next morning to find that Lucy, who shared her bed, was already up and gone.

Emily threw back her covers and hurriedly dressed. With her shoes in one hand, she tiptoed down the hallway, past closed doors that muffled the sound of snoring.

"Good morning," she caroled, stepping into the kitchen.

At the table, Moses was drinking a cup of milk and eating pancakes. He nodded, his eyes meeting hers just briefly before looking away. Lucy stood at the iron stove, flipping pancakes with a grim look on her face. "Morning," Lucy said.

Emily worked the pump handle at the sink. "I thought I'd be the first one awake, but you beat me again, Lucy."

Water splashed into a basin with a cold, metallic ring. Holding her breath, Emily squeezed her eyes shut tight and plunged her face into the water. "Ahh!" she shrieked, jerking upright and dripping water down her dress. She laughed breathlessly and reached for a flour-sack towel. As she scrubbed her face, she looked from Lucy to Moses and back again. "Do I get any of those 'cakes, or does Moses claim every one of them?"

"No, ma'am," Moses said, wide-eyed and rising so abruptly from the table that he knocked his chair over. He opened his mouth to apologize, and then shut it.

"Don't fuss yourself," Lucy said, bending down to right the chair. She touched his arm lightly.

Emily blinked in surprise. "Well, my gracious, what a fuss. I only asked if I could have some, too, Moses. You don't need to tear out of here like the devil's after you."

"No, ma'am," he said, slowly sitting down again.

Emily took the coffeepot from the back of the stove, poured herself a cup, and then sat opposite Moses. She waited for him to look up so she could give him a smile. The least she could do was let him know he wasn't a slave in the MacKenzies' kitchen. But he kept his face turned down, eating with a hurried air, as though he expected Emily to snatch his breakfast away at any moment.

"You can have as many as you can eat," she assured him. "I myself can eat a dozen or two at once."

Moses suddenly laughed and raised his eyes to her face. Then Emily noticed the cut on his lip.

"Say, how did you do that?" she asked. "I cut my lip once walking into a door. I was arguing with Lucy at the time, that's why I didn't notice the door being shut. Is that what you did?"

Moses didn't answer. He put his fork down, rubbing his palms on his knees.

"It was a door called Mr. Stockwell," Lucy spoke up, clattering pans together on the stove.

"What?" Emily turned around. "You mean he *hit* Moses?"

"That's right," Lucy said bitterly.

"What a brute he is!" Emily said in disgust. "Look here, Moses, you just eat as many pancakes as you can, and if that lip hurts, you just pour on more maple syrup."

"Thank you, miss," he replied.

"What makes you think syrup will help?" Lucy muttered as Emily rose from the table.

Emily wiped a stray drop of water off her cheek and shrugged. The tone of Lucy's voice made her feel guilty, but she didn't know what she'd done wrong. Ever since the Stockwells had arrived, Lucy had been acting as if she had a toothache.

"Well, it might," Emily said stubbornly. "It always makes me feel better."

Lucy turned and gave Emily a long, skeptical look. Then, as a scorched smell rose from the pan, she broke her gaze away. Emily watched Lucy flip a pancake and wished she could think of something to say.

"Good morning," Lavinia said, waddling into the kitchen with a full basket of linen in her arms. "Emily, these napkins are terribly soiled. See what you can do about them, won't you?"

Emily took the basket from her sister and backed out

of the kitchen, going through the lean-to shed that led to the side garden.

"Be sure to get them truly clean!" Lavinia called after her anxiously. "I'm just sure that Mrs. Stockwell will find a stain."

"Oh, I will!" Emily shouted. She pushed the outer door open with her foot and made a face to herself. "I wish those Stockwells would weigh anchor and go."

With a grimace, she hoisted the laundry basket onto the trestle table in the yard and looked up at the crazy quilt of angles and pitches that made up the inn's roofs. A gull stood on the peak of a dormer, its shoulders hunched, its black-currant eyes fixed sourly on her. Suddenly it let out one cranky scream and flapped away, out toward the harbor.

"I know just what you mean," Emily grumbled, and headed back into the house to begin heating water.

Lucy was alone in the kitchen, frying eggs. Emily went to her at the stove and looked down into the pan. Lucy prodded the egg yolks with a fork to test their firmness as the grease popped and sizzled. Her shoulders were rigid.

"Are you sore with me?" Emily asked. "Because if you are, I don't know why."

"No." Lucy let her breath out in a long sigh. "It ain't you I'm sore at."

"Honor bright?" Emily pressed with a hopeful lift in her heart. "I didn't somehow do you a bad turn when I wasn't noticing?"

Lucy gave her a crooked smile. "You never did anyone a bad turn and you know it."

"Well, I admit I'm careless," Emily said, going to the sink and pumping water into a pail to fill the huge kettles. She raised her voice over the gushing. "I just hate to see you getting vaporish. I'm glad it was nothing."

"It wasn't nothing." Lucy slid the eggs out of the pan onto a platter of bacon, and set the platter on a tray. "I don't call Moses being hit for no reason nothing."

Emily looked at her friend, feeling contrite. "I know, nor do I, and I know you always want to help the helpless. These people are tossing us head over heels, and I don't like it any more than you do, but they won't be here long, Lucy. We'll be back to our regular ways."

"For some people, regular ways are hard and bitter ways," Lucy said. "That sounds pretty irregular to me." Without another word, she carried the food out of the kitchen, and the door swung shut behind her.

Emily turned back to the pump handle and worked it slowly, thinking of the cut on Moses's lip. She rubbed her own lip with the back of her hand, and then shook her head, banishing the uncomfortable image from her mind.

Emily's arms were slippery with soap and bluing two hours later as she cranked the handle of the huge, clumsy mangle. The wringer clanked and squealed like some demonic machine in its death throes. Water dribbled through the rollers, and the contraption spat a napkin, squeezed pitifully flat, into Emily's waiting hand. She spread it apart by the corners, inspected it for stains, and then tossed it into a tub of milky starch.

"Whew," she said, pushing a wisp of hair off her forehead and gazing up at the sky. Laundering was always backbreaking work, and she loathed it even more than translating Latin. She felt a breath of wind on her cheek, and pictured the *Rosy*, sails bellied out, prow leaping keenly through the waves.

"You look like an oil painting by one of those Europeans," came a voice. " 'The Pretty Washer Maid.' "

Emily spun around. Blount Stockwell was leaning against the side of the house, regarding her with a friendly smile as he sketched her.

"You think this is quaint, do you?" Emily asked, hearing him say "pretty" again in her mind and burning to see her portrait. She held up her hands. "Look here, I'm so shriveled I look like a little old lady I know called Granny Godwin. And *she* has so many wrinkles on her that she looks like an applehead doll."

Blount laughed, a rich, carefree sound that made a gull flying overhead dip down to look him over. Emily suddenly wondered what her hair looked like, and had a dread certainty that it was falling down her back in a damp and hopeless tangle. Her dress was darkened in large patches where soapsuds had slopped over her.

"I suppose you think being soaking wet is my natural state," she said with some embarrassment. "After the way I appeared yesterday, and now today."

"Well, I did wonder," Blount said, pushing himself

away from the building and strolling toward her. "But I assumed it had something to do with you Marbleheaders' fondness for boats and the ocean."

"That must be it," Emily said. "Whenever I see water I have an overmastering compulsion to throw myself into it."

"I hoped you might say so," he replied, his soft Southern pronunciation sounding strange and interesting to Emily's ears.

He looked down into the washtubs and then looked up again, a mischievous gleam in his eyes. "I thought I could convince you to abandon your chores and start our sailing lessons."

Emily tugged the strings of her apron. "You just convinced me," she said, yanking off her apron and hanging it on the mangle.

"You won't catch any trouble on my account, now, will you?" he asked.

She glanced at the side door of the house and wondered briefly what Lavinia would say about her slipping out. But the napkins and tablecloths would be all the brighter and cleaner for a long soak, and all the more likely to please the Stockwells.

And if it came to that, she would be busy making one of the Stockwells welcome, so Lavinia would hardly have cause to complain.

"Trouble?" Emily snapped her fingers. "Not a bit. But it'll cost you."

"Any price would be a bargain," Blount returned without hesitation.

Emily grinned. "You'll have to show me that sketch you did of me. Nobody ever took my likeness before."

"I don't know why. You're a perfect subject." Blount held his sketchbook out to her.

The sassy smile faded from Emily's lips as she inspected the portrait. He had drawn her quickly, with a graceful economy of line. But he had captured her image with skill, even to the upward glance of her eyes, yearning toward the sky. She felt a strange sensation of having been opened up and put back together again.

"You're quite an artist," she said uncomfortably.

Blount made a dismissing motion with his hand. "It's nothing. Only something to occupy myself," he said, tossing the book onto the grass. "Now, for the open ocean."

"You'll have to settle for sheltered harbor, at first," Emily said with a laugh. She struck out toward the garden gate, already judging the strength and direction of the wind. Then she noticed that Blount hadn't followed her.

"Coming?" she asked, looking back.

"Oh." Blount hurried to join her. "I thought you might need to change your dress."

Emily's eyebrows arched high. "I'm sorry to disappoint you, but I don't have any special yachting costume," she said. "Laundry, sailing—I get wet no matter what, so it doesn't much make a difference what I wear, does it?"

For a moment, Blount gaped at her, dumbfounded. Then his face broke into another wide smile, and he made her a bow. "A woman who wears such confidence is the best-dressed woman in town," he declared.

"Thank you very much," Emily said, keeping a straight face with difficulty. "I'm very complimented."

He looked at her, his eyes puzzled but amused, as though he didn't quite know what to make of her. Emily looked straight back at him and decided that his eyes were the most handsome brown she had ever seen. She remembered how provoked she had been the night before, and decided that Blount beat Micah hands down for charm and pleasantness. Blount was a pleasure to talk with, whereas Micah never said a word that wasn't as barbed as a harpoon.

"Shall we?" Blount asked, holding out his arm. A butterfly hovering over the tangle of rose vines lit on his elbow.

Emily laughed and shooed it away. She knew enough to take his arm as she'd seen ladies do, although she had always thought it was a silly convention. But tucking her hand in the crook of his arm and looking up at his profile, she decided that there was good reason for it, at that.

"Why, thank you," she said, hiding her surprise as he steered her around a mud puddle. The street made a sharp jog to the left, and two alleys crisscrossed it at odd angles. Hollyhocks stood sentry outside narrow doors, and a cat, sunning itself on a granite step, rolled lazily over and toppled off. It blinked and promptly began washing itself with a great show of dignity. Emily giggled.

"I hope you won't be offended, Miss MacKenzie," Blount began. "But I think this is the queerest little town I've ever been in. It's as crooked as an apple tree."

"I don't know if I should be offended or not," Emily replied. "If you consider an apple tree an ugly thing—"

"I consider it a delightful thing," he broke in. "And I —oh, here, allow me."

He ushered her carefully around a pair of dogs quarreling over a lobster claw. Emily had never before been treated with such delicacy and was tempted to tease him for it. But then, up ahead, she saw Celia and Madeleine strolling toward them, arm in arm in gossip. Suppressing a grin, Emily tucked her hand a bit more firmly through Blount's arm and looked up at him with a smile. He smiled back at her.

"Yoo-hoo! Good morning, Emily," Celia called across the street.

"Good morning, Emily," Madeleine echoed.

Both girls stared unabashedly at Blount, and Emily turned to wave at them. "Oh, hello, Celia, Madeleine."

Blount smiled and nodded in greeting. Emily lowered her head and pressed her lips together to keep from laughing as they continued on. She glanced back once and was delighted to see the two girls standing in the street, their mouths gaping open.

"I think we're going to have a lovely day, don't you?" Emily asked Blount.

"It's already a treat," he replied.

She laughed, feeling extremely grown-up and worldly, and led the way through another alley. They turned a corner, and there was the Little Harbor spread before them. Blount stopped to look, and Emily stood beside him, enjoying the familiar view through his eyes.

Small boats bobbed at their moorings or bumped cozily against the docks while gulls and kittiwakes strutted importantly up and down the piers as though they had business. Fishermen with leathery faces repaired nets or stacked crates, and the air was filled with the mingled scents of paint, tar, salt, and fish. Over it all arched the fine blue heavens: the sun blazed gloriously, and the breeze whispered in their ears.

Blount stood as though enchanted, a smile on his lips and an eager light in his eyes. As Emily looked up at him, enjoying his enjoyment, a sudden thump behind her ribs set her heart knocking. She turned away, cheeks pink, and busied herself with her hair, trying to wrestle it into some kind of order.

"This is wonderful," Blount said at last.

"Do you think so?" Emily said indistinctly. She drew a deep breath and looked up at him again. Her heart behaved itself. "Come along, then."

She led the way out onto the dock. "Here's my—"

"Wait, let me guess which is your boat," Blount begged. He looked this way and that, his face flushed with anticipation and his brown hair lifting off his forehead in the breeze. "I'm sure I can tell."

"I'm sure you can't," Emily said with a laugh.

He pointed to a sleek, blue-hulled sailboat at a mooring twenty feet away. "It must be that one. It's the prettiest ship in sight."

Emily's face fell. "It's not a ship," she mumbled. She gestured weakly toward the *Rosy*, which looked small and lumpish compared to the blue craft. "This is mine."

"This?" Blount stood back for a better look.

"Don't you like her?" Emily asked.

Blount gave her a heart-stopping smile. "I like her very much." His gaze lingered on Emily for a moment. Then he looked at the *Rosy* again. "It looks like just the boat for me to learn in."

Flustered, Emily hopped down into the boat and worked with scattered concentration on a knot. "If you'll just come aboard," she said.

"Aye aye, Captain." He saluted, and stepped down onto the gunwale.

"No!"

The *Rosy* pitched, and Blount waved his arms wildly to regain his balance before falling in an ungainly heap at the bottom of the boat. Emily stared in horror as the boat rocked Blount back and forth.

"First mistake." Blount groaned.

"Oh, gracious." Emily met his eyes and spluttered with laughter. "Oh, dear. Are you hurt?"

"Only in my dignity," he said, pulling himself up. "I reckon I was fairly stupid just then, but please don't keel-haul me."

Emily managed a solemn nod. "We MacKenzies make it a practice not to keelhaul our guests."

"Thank goodness for that." Blount rubbed his head. "You aren't ready to give up on me, are you?"

"I'm not quite sure if you have the makings of a sailor," Emily began slowly.

"But under your guidance I'll become a buccaneer," Blount insisted. "I have every confidence in you."

Emily smiled again and continued unfurling the sail. "That's very nice of you to say, but if you suffer one more injury before we leave the dock . . ."

"I will remain unscathed," Blount promised, one hand over his heart. "Now, what do I do first?"

"Your first lesson is to learn how to move around a boat," Emily said firmly. "Now, you sit there by the tiller —yes, that stick thing in the back—and you decide which way the wind is blowing while I hoist the sail."

Blount stood up and dutifully did as he was bid, picking his careful way to the stern and manning the tiller. Although Emily had her back to him, she was quite certain he was watching her every move. She was glad the wind was so strong: it made a sound reason for the color in her cheeks.

"Now," she said, casting off the bow and stern lines and taking a seat beside him as the *Rosy* began to drift away from the dock. "Which way did you say the wind was blowing?"

Blount licked one finger and held it up, first facing one way, and then another. He licked his finger again, frowned, and turned in yet another direction. "I . . ."

Emily grinned and pointed at a distant flag riffling in the breeze.

"I must look fairly pitiful to you," Blount said.

"Don't worry. You'll learn fast."

"So now that we know where the wind is, we let it push us, is that it?" Blount asked.

"Push us?" Emily repeated. "The wind is coming

from there." She pointed toward the mouth of the harbor. "And that is where I aim to go. Now hold on to your hat."

"I haven't got a hat."

"Then hold on to your head." Emily close-hauled the *Rosy* to beat hard up into the wind. The boat sprinted forward, sending up a glittering wake.

"The wind is pulling us!" Blount exclaimed, gripping the gunwales. "It's tremendous!"

Emily laughed, shook her hair out of her eyes, and caught the mainsheet more firmly in her hand. "Take the tiller," she shouted above the rush of the wind.

He looked at her with such delight and excitement in his eyes that Emily laughed again. "First lesson!" she called. "Tell the wind where you want to go and make it take you there!"

For twenty minutes, Emily showed off shamelessly, putting the *Rosy* through her paces. At first, she was aiming to impress Blount, and kept one eye out to gauge his reaction to everything she did. But soon she had forgotten all about him, absorbed in the joy of skimming across the water like a ray of light. At last, Emily steered the sailboat into the lee of a headland, and loosened the sail to slow down.

She smiled at Blount. "Wasn't that glorious fun?"

Blount's hair was windblown and tousled all around his head, and his eyes glinted brilliantly. He let out an astonished laugh.

"Are you sure you aren't some kind of mermaid or sea witch?" he asked, catching his breath.

Emily shook her head with a smile, constantly giving

and taking with the tiller and mainsail sheet at every changing whim of the wind.

"It is true, most 'Headers are more at home on the water than off it," she told him. "My own great-grandfather, Lieutenant John MacKenzie, had saltwater in his veins. He was in General Glover's Marblehead Militia that rowed Washington across the Delaware. My great-grandfather sat behind the general and rowed like blazes, and he knew how, for he spent his youth smuggling rum and molasses in these waters and outwitting the British."

"It was Marblehead men that took Washington to victory?" Blount asked, his eyes wide.

Emily shrugged. "Oh, yes, when you need a war won or a ship sailed or a fish caught, everyone comes to us."

Blount was gazing around at the rocky shores, where the waves pooled in foamy currents and weeds streamed up and down with the tide. Shellfish clung to the rocks like bunches of wet, stony grapes, and across the top of a cliff, a dog ran joyously back and forth, barking at the shrieking seabirds.

"I'm out of my element here," Blount said, shaking his head. "You Yankees live in a difficult and dangerous place, yet you all seem so capable. It makes me feel as though I can't do the simplest thing. Our darkies do everything for us. You see, they—"

"Look over there," Emily interrupted. Her heart had lurched at the word "darkies." "That's Peach's Point. They say it got its name from a man named Peach who lived at the tip of the land in a barrel. Now, how's that for a queer little place?"

"It may be queer, but it's beautiful," Blount said.

Emily nodded and concentrated on tacking around.

"I've upset you, haven't I?" Blount asked. "I'm sorry, what did I say?"

"It's nothing," Emily mumbled, and instantly regretted that she had not challenged him. She knew she had done a dishonorable thing. Frowning, she turned to look at him while the wind pushed her hair back from her forehead and fanned her hot face.

"I want to remind you that Lucy is my sister, even if she isn't related by flesh and blood," Emily said. "I would be very glad if you didn't discuss your slaves when you're with me."

Blount nodded gravely. "I won't, then, if you ask me not to."

"I do," Emily said, glad of his willing acceptance. "It's a necessary condition of sailing in this boat."

"That's fine, Miss MacKenzie," Blount told her with an easy smile. "Lucy must be a wonderful girl to inspire such faithfulness from you. I admire your loyalty. I admire you."

Flattered, Emily smiled back at him. "Oh, thank you," she murmured self-consciously. She took the tiller and steered for the harbor, blushing with confusion the whole way.

# Chapter Five

WHEN SHE HAD finished her chores for the evening, Emily climbed the stairs to her bedroom at the front of the house, changed into her nightdress, and then threw open the window to lean out into the night. The air from the harbor was still as fresh as it had been at noon and she breathed in deeply, feeling the balminess against her skin. Laughter drifted up from the tavern below; a voice from far down the dark street said "Good night, Ma," and a door closed. Emily smiled, resting her head against the window frame, and fingered the lace at her throat. She wondered what Blount was doing down the hall in his room.

The door behind her opened, and Lucy came in with a softly burning lamp in her hand. As she set it on a table a large moth blundered in through the open window and hovered around the light.

Emily yawned. "I'm so tired I could sleep standing up," she said, turning back the covers on their bed.

"Sailing is tiring work," Lucy teased.

"It certainly is. Maybe I'd have been more refreshed scrubbing floors all day long." Emily climbed up onto the tall bed, which crackled and whispered as the cornshucks shifted in the mattress.

Lucy began to undress, and hung her clothes in their wardrobe. "Moses says sometimes he gets so tired he does sleep standing up."

"I'd like to see that," Emily said with a giggle. "Some of the boys go out at night to tip cows over. The cows sleep standing in the pasture, and it only takes a shove to topple them."

"Moses ain't a cow," Lucy said gravely.

"I know." Emily shifted on the bed. "I didn't mean he was."

Above the lamp, the moth smacked against the glass chimney and into the wall, and a fine dusting of wing powder drifted through the lamplight. Emily waved the moth away, but it kept circling the light. She watched it, feeling her body relax, letting sleep fill the corners of the room.

"He told me today he has to stay up until Mr. Stockwell goes to bed, no matter what time it is," Lucy added.

Emily's gaze was fixed on the moth. "Who does? Blount?" she asked sleepily.

"No, Moses," Lucy said, climbing onto the bed. "Even when he was a child, just standing by the door in case he was needed." She shook her head. "It's not right to do that to a child."

"No, I don't guess it is," Emily agreed. She wriggled

57

her way down into the covers and pressed her cheek to the pillow. From there, she gazed up at Lucy's profile.

"He's very strong, though," Lucy continued, tucking her knees up. "He split a pile of kindling for me this afternoon and hardly broke a sweat."

"Mmm." Emily closed her eyes. "I reckon that means he's no cow, but he's strong as a bull."

Lucy chuckled softly. "That's right. But gentle, too. And he has marvelous eyes. I never saw such eyes, like he's filled with pain but won't say a word of complaint."

Instantly, Emily was wide awake. "Lucy?"

"Yes?"

Emily put her hand on her friend's arm. "Lucy, you ain't going sweet on Moses, are you?"

"What if I am?"

"But, Lucy." Emily propped herself up on her elbow. Behind Lucy's head, the flitting moth made wild shadows on the wall. "Lucy, you be careful. They'll be leaving soon, so you shouldn't go getting foolish over that boy."

Lucy plucked at the coverlet but said nothing.

"And besides," Emily continued, glancing at the door. "Don't forget you're free and he ain't."

"That's not a thing I'm likely to forget, is it?" Lucy asked, looking evenly at Emily.

They stared at one another for a long, quiet moment, the only sound was the moth batting against the lamp. A whisper of apprehension stole up Emily's spine. In her mind's eye she saw Moses as a little boy, standing in a Virginia parlor, struggling to keep awake, yearning for a bed that was not his to own, and unable to speak a word of protest. She saw the rising and falling strokes of an ax melt into the rising and falling lashes of a riding crop against a young man's brown-skinned back. Moses was a slave. A slave. She thought of Mr. Stockwell's heavy hand, and Emily suddenly felt sickened.

"Lucy," she whispered. "Lucy, you be careful. I know you want to be kind to him, but stay clear."

Lucy stared across the room into the shadows, her forehead creased.

"Lucy, please," Emily whispered.

A faint smile turned up one corner of Lucy's mouth. "Don't you worry about me," she said, and leaned over and blew out the lamp.

Emily stared into the sudden darkness, trying to see her sister. She heard the heavy body of the moth batter against the hot lamp chimney again before it dropped to the floor and was still.


Lucy was gone when Emily awoke at dawn. "You fool," Emily muttered, dragging on a calico dress and digging her toes into her shoes. "I wanted to talk to you."

She hastened down the hallway, fingering her buttons into place and patting her unruly brown hair. Underfoot, the broad chestnut floorboards creaked like ship's rigging.

At the landing, she stopped to look through the window. In the yard, by one of the long, low outbuildings, Lucy and Moses were standing together. While Emily watched, Lucy threw her head back and laughed, and the first rays of the sun fell across her long bare throat. A flush heated Emily's face, and she nearly tripped over her hem in her hurry to get downstairs.

"Lavinia," Emily said, bursting into the kitchen. She looked around to be sure they were alone.

"Yes," Lavinia said. She leaned over to peer into the firebox of the stove, and then rattled the poker around inside. "Fetch me some coal, Em."

"I will, but I have to speak with you first," Emily said, taking a peek out the door. She shut it firmly behind her and faced her sister. "Lucy is setting her cap at Moses. I just know it."

Lavinia straightened, one hand at her back. When she frowned, two deep furrows went from her nose to the sides of her mouth. "What?"

"I'm sure that Lucy is getting to be a little bit in love with Moses," Emily whispered. "Or maybe even more than a little. Now, I ask you, is that sensible?"

"Sensible, no," Lavinia said. She put her arms around her belly, cradling her unborn baby. "I fear love never is sensible, or I'd never have married a whaling man."

"But at least Zachary ain't—" Emily cast a quick look out the open window. "At least he ain't a *slave*."

Lavinia lowered herself into a chair and wiped her hands on her apron. There was a sheen of sweat on her forehead. "That's true," she said faintly.

"So we can't let Lucy be in love with Moses," Emily pressed. She felt a flutter under her ribs as she looked at her sister. "Don't you agree?"

"Yes." Lavinia sighed. "And Mr. Stockwell is not

60

likely to be pleased about it, either. Make sure Lucy stays out of his way, in case he gets an itch to hit someone."

"If he hits her, I'll harpoon him!" Emily cried out.

Lavinia closed her eyes for a moment. "Emily, please don't be so impetuous," she pleaded in a weak voice.

Emily crossed the kitchen and took Lavinia's hand. "Are you feeling bad, Lavvy?"

"No." Lavinia licked her lips, and then looked up shamefacedly at Emily. "Well, a bit, I am."

Emily pulled a chair close and sat down. "Now, I don't want you to worry about anything," she said firmly. "I won't harpoon Mr. Stockwell, I promise. But I'll make sure Lucy steers clear of him—and Moses. There's plenty of Negro families with boys around here. Why does she have to go liking a slave? That's just like her to be so contrary. She just can't see a hurt thing without wanting to mother it."

"Where's Father?"

"I don't know," Emily said. "Are you certain you won't go back to bed?"

"No, don't be a goose." Lavinia managed a laugh and rose clumsily to her feet. "I'm only feeling the heat, that's all. Now, go along, find Father and tell him I need him."

"But why?" Emily asked.

"Never you mind," Lavinia said, smiling tenderly. "Inquisitiveness in young ladies is not an attractive quality."

"Oh, pooh," Emily retorted.

Lavinia moved back to the stove and retied her apron more securely. Emily watched her for a moment, determined to save her sister from anxiety if she could. She lugged the coal scuttle to the stove and tossed in several handfuls. Then, with a decisive nod, she turned and marched out the back door.

Emily strode through the garden, her skirts swishing busily, brushing past lavender and tansy and chamomile. A bird twittered and then burst up from the grass in a flurry of wings. Emily paused to follow it with her eyes. When she turned back to the path, Moses was walking toward her, carrying a basket.

"Morning, miss," Moses said with a glimmer of a smile.

"Good morning, Moses." Emily fidgeted with her apron. "I'm glad I ran into you. I—I wanted to—" She trailed off, feeling pompous and foolish.

Moses waited. Emily was only too aware that he did have beautiful eyes, just as Lucy had said, and that his hands were long and finely formed, although rough from heavy work. She glanced into the basket and saw two brown eggs.

"We've only got one hen that lays brown eggs," she said, startled. "Why, you didn't find where that hen's been laying, did you? That is the sneakingest bird I ever knew. I hardly ever can find her eggs."

Moses lifted the basket and touched the eggs delicately. Then he lifted his eyes to her and grinned. "Just patience, that's all it takes. She'll show you. She gets to busying around and soon she forgets all about you setting there, and she goes to the eggs. You just set and wait quietly."

"I admit, sitting and waiting quietly is something I never learned," Emily said with a laugh.

"I learned it long ago," Moses replied, looking up over the rooftops. "Didn't King Jesus say—just you wait patiently and the kingdom of heaven is going to be yours?"

Emily sighed, feeling suddenly sad. "Yes, something like that, I guess." She shuffled one foot in the dust of the path, shaking her head. "Seems too bad it won't come until we die, though."

"That's something I can wait patiently for," Moses said. "I guess I'm not in no hurry for it, but I'll be glad when I get there. And I do believe I'll get there by and by." Moses smiled at her.

"I'm sure my mother did, and I hope I do," Emily said. "But sometimes I fear I'm just too bad and irreligious."

"I doubt you are."

Emily cocked her head. "You seem plenty certain."

"Lucy says you got a heart of gold," Moses replied.

Emily's heart thumped as she recalled why she had stopped Moses in the first place. Lucy.

But at the moment she didn't have it in her to warn Moses off.

"Was there something you were wanting me for?" Moses asked, shifting his hold on the basket of fragile eggs.

"No," Emily said. "I guess not."

He nodded and stepped around her to go indoors. Emily stood alone on the path, staring down at the drops of dew on the face of a Johnny-jump-up. She was mildly astonished to have had a philosophical discussion so early in the morning, and with a slave named Moses. And she felt a mystifying sense of sadness over Lucy. For several moments, Emily stayed where she was, not thinking of anything in particular, but feeling a wordless welling of anger in her heart.

Then she heard the crackle of a twig breaking underfoot on the path behind her.

"I hardly ever rise this early, but I have to say it's a nice time of the day, cool and pretty," came Blount's voice. "Just like Miss MacKenzie."

Emily spun around. "What do you need slaves for, anyway?" she demanded.

He stepped backward in surprise. "I beg your pardon?"

"I guess you heard me," Emily said. "Why do you need them?"

"You are very direct," Blount began slowly. "Just yesterday you said you didn't care to discuss it."

"That was yesterday," Emily said, hands on her hips. "Can you answer me direct?"

He nodded, and met her gaze without flinching. "Yes, I can. But could we walk a bit?"

Emily went to the gate, but Blount was there first and opened it for her. She nodded formally and passed through ahead of him.

Blount clasped his hands behind his back and paced by her side, a frown creasing his forehead. "I agree with

64

you, with many Yankees, that slavery is a mighty sorrow-ful institution."

"Yes," Emily prompted. She made herself look away from his handsome profile and keep her mind fixed on the question. She saw that he was leading them toward the Little Harbor and that he was in no hurry to speak.

When they arrived at the harbor, he stopped and looked out at the sparkling water. The fishing boats had gone long before sunrise, and the port was quiet, a haven for the gulls that rode the gentle waves. Emily waited.

"The Bible tells us plainly that what we do is wrong," Blount confessed. He squinted in the fresh, horizontal light, gazing out to sea, and let out a regretful sigh. "If my ancestors had never bought slaves, if the black man had never set foot on these shores, I would be very very thankful."

"And yet your family owns slaves."

"They are here," he continued. "And if we did not rule them, guide them, protect them—they would fall into ruin."

Emily gaped at him. "But why do you say that?"

"The Negro race is a naturally inferior one," Blount explained. "This has been proven time and time again by modern science. They simply do not have the capacity for learning, for self-governance, and for self-control."

"Fiddlesticks," Emily said, striking out across the pebbly, littered boatyard toward the docks. "Lucy is as smart as a whip. Why, she learned her lessons faster than I did usually, and she still keeps at it even though we don't attend school any longer."

Blount, keeping pace with her on the dock, shrugged. "There are always exceptions," he said, brushing aside a lock of hair that blew into his eyes. "The ones that stand out from the herd."

"Lucy ain't a cow," Emily said sullenly. She looked down at the *Rosy* bumping gently against the dock. "She's a girl and she's my sister."

"Now I've hurt your feelings, and I swear I never meant to do that," Blount said, taking her hand and pressing it between his own. He met her eyes intently. "I would never want to hurt you. Please accept my apology."

"Well, I . . ." Emily faltered. "Well, I don't know if I should." She pulled her hand from his and turned away, letting the breeze cool her flushed cheeks.

Blount shook his head. "Miss MacKenzie, you are not like other girls I know."

"That's lucky for you, I guess," Emily muttered.

"No, I feel I've been missing out something special," Blount corrected her. "The girls in Virginia are full of wiles and stratagems, as though their thoughts were a puzzle one is required to solve. You, on the other hand, are completely forthright."

Emily sniffed and shrugged one shoulder.

"You are the most able, the most adept—"

"If you want to flatter me, you might as well not liken me to a deckhand," Emily broke in.

He laughed richly, and she turned away to hide a smile. Her gaze settled on her sailboat.

"I supposed the girls in Virginia wouldn't know the

first thing about handling a boat," she said with sneaking pride.

"Not the first thing, nor the last," Blount agreed. "Mostly they act as though the slightest little puff of wind would hasten them to their graves."

"They sound a useless bunch," Emily said.

Blount grinned, and raised one limp hand to his forehead. "What, me go in a dreadful boat?" he exclaimed in a falsetto voice. "My land, what if I see a fish?"

Emily laughed. "I'd like to see them spot a right whale!"

"Oh, my land!" Blount cried, shrinking back in alarm.

Emily's eyes danced with amusement. "Merciful heavens," she drawled. "Whatever shall I do?"

"I don't know about you," Blount gasped. "But I declare I'll swoon! Somebody catch me!"

To Emily's amazement, Blount actually stumbled backward and collapsed in a heap on the dock. He lay there, eyes closed, one hand on his heart and one over his brow while Emily crowed with laughter. She looked down at him, and he opened one eye.

"I was hoping you might leap out to catch me," he teased. "I could imagine it so well."

Blushing fiercely, Emily turned away. She didn't know if he meant to compliment her or to ridicule her ungirlish capabilities.

"If that's your idea of imagination, then you are likely to be disappointed," she said with spirit. "You're a good six inches taller than I am, and I'd fall over myself if I tried."

"Maybe I'll try it again," he said.

He stood up beside her, and resumed his mocking portrayal. "Somebody catch me!" he cried faintly.

Without more warning, he began falling toward Emily, who let out a shriek and jumped to one side. Blount's eyes flew open in dismay as he found himself toppling off the deck.

"Blount!" Emily gasped. "Oh no!"

He plunged into the shallow seawater and lay facedown and motionless. Bubbles broke quietly around his head.

"Now, that's enough fooling," Emily said.

He didn't move. The swells bobbed him up and down.

"Blount?" she called, kneeling and stretching a hand anxiously for the floating tails of his coat. *"Blount?"*

With a surging splash, he drew himself up and flung the wet hair back off his forehead. He stood waist-deep next to the dock, smiling up at her as the water streamed from his once-elegant clothes. Emily drew back, relieved and embarrassed and wanting ridiculously to fall into the water with him.

"You do care, Captain," he said, catching his breath. "You've brought me back from the brink of death."

Emily's heart was beating wildly. "You scoundrel," she said, dashing her hand through the water to splash him. "Stop calling me Captain. You're only mocking me. I think I should have let you drown."

He laughed, and his brown eyes gleamed. "Would you have been sad if I did?"

She tried not to smile. "Perhaps."

"Then it would have been worth it," Blount replied with a sweeping, watery bow. "To know I touched your heart, I would die content."

"Is everyone in Virginia as crazy as you are?" Emily asked as she stood up.

"Only the ones who've met Emily MacKenzie."

"Then it's lucky for Virginia only one of them has," Emily said, turning on her heel and striding back toward the boatyard.

"No," Blount called after her. "Lucky for me."

She paused for a moment and pressed one hand to her cheek. Then she hurried away from the harbor and Blount's laugh.

Almost out of breath, Emily rounded the corner of a building and ran full tilt into Micah. He grabbed her arms for support and for a moment they teetered together like two drunkards, before Emily pulled herself upright.

"Thank you," she said, lifting her chin. "You can stop squeezing the life out of me now."

Micah let go of her and bent to pick his hat up off the ground. "I guess I'm supposed to beg your pardon when you ram into me," he said wryly.

Emily flushed. "Excuse me," she replied. She watched him with growing indignation as he brushed his hat brim. "It isn't exactly courteous to call attention to a fault in manners, is it, Micah?"

"Well if it isn't, why did you just do it?" he asked, quirking one eyebrow.

Her face colored even pinker. "Micah, I should have thought that with all the society patrons crowding the Ship, more of their graces would have rubbed off on you. I have recently had experience of the way a real gentleman behaves, and I think I should tell you that you—that you—" She stammered in exasperation, seeing the glint of laughter in his eyes.

"I can hardly wait to hear this," Micah said. "But I have an appointment. And I expect Lavinia's needing you at home. How is your sister? Almost near her confinement?"

"I—why—" Emily spluttered.

"Good-bye."

He tilted his hat at an angle and sauntered away.

Emily glared at his back, guiltily aware that she had left Lavinia without word, and hating Micah for reminding her of it.

Scowling, she stalked home, her skirts flapping like sails. "Lavinia!" she called, striding through the empty kitchen. "I'm back! I only stepped out for a moment!"

She went through the kitchen into the hallway, drawn by the sound of voices. "Lavinia?"

When she turned the corner, she came upon her sister and Mr. Stockwell at the bottom of the stairs. Lavinia's face was pale and set.

"This is the very thing I have been complaining about," Mr. Stockwell said, every line in his face sour with bad temper. "There is a great deal of unmannerly noise in this establishment."

"I do beg your pardon," Lavinia said. "Its being built right on the street is what makes it so loud. We get all the noise of traffic, carriages—"

"I notice you don't mention the clamoring of rude girls," Mr. Stockwell said.

Emily's face blazed. She looked for support from Lavinia, but her sister was bent on appeasing the man.

"Sir, my sister is young."

"And the young are thoughtless," Mr. Stockwell said coldly. "Nor do they seem to know their proper place."

Lavinia's expression hardened. "Sir?"

"I do not intend for my son to become entrapped by a parlor maid."

Emily drew a deep breath to explode, but Lavinia cut her off. "My sister is only giving your son sailing lessons at his own request," she said with a coldness that matched his own. "And at the sacrifice of her regular chores. I assure you, you need have absolutely no fear that our families could ever be in any way allied."

Astonished, Emily gaped at her sister, and Mr. Stockwell himself seemed momentarily nonplussed.

Then he drew himself up. "I suppose I can't expect more consideration in an establishment such as this one, but if it isn't too much to ask, my wife will require breakfast in her room this morning."

"I'll get it," Lavinia said evenly.

"No, you won't, Lavvy," Emily said, putting her arm around Lavinia's shoulders and glaring at Mr. Stockwell.

71

"I'll get it. I know it ain't polite to mention such indelicate things, but you may notice my sister is in no condition to be carrying trays up and down stairs."

Mr. Stockwell tipped his head back and looked down his nose at them. "It makes no difference to me who gets it," he said, starting back up the stairs with a heavy tread. "As long as it *gets* gotten."

"I wish your wife would get it herself," Emily muttered under her breath. "She's no sicker than I am. I'm sure she just plays at it to get attention and make a nuisance of herself."

"Emily, please," Lavinia whispered. She waited until the sound of a door closing upstairs reached them, and then put her hands on Emily's shoulders. "Don't make things any worse."

"Why not?" Emily growled, only slightly regretting her rudeness. "I noticed you gave him a pretty fair set down yourself."

"His suggestion was despicable." Lavinia shook her head. "I don't know, Emily. I almost wish they would go. Their being here is hard on all of us."

"Well, I wouldn't mind if they moved to a different hotel," Emily declared.

"Then you'd miss your sailing companion, wouldn't you?" Lavinia teased, her blue eyes warm in spite of her fatigue.

"Oh, I wouldn't even notice he was gone," Emily said.

"I'm glad of that," Lavinia said. "I'd like to think you

had enough scruples not to keep company with a boy whose father owns slaves."

Emily blushed. "He's really not a bit like his father, Lavvy. But I still wouldn't care if they left," she insisted hastily.

"That's fine."

Lavinia patted Emily's cheek and headed toward the kitchen, leaving Emily with a frown puckering her forehead.

"He's really not at all like them," she repeated to herself slowly. Still frowning, she followed her sister to the kitchen to fetch Mrs. Stockwell's breakfast.

# Chapter Six

SIX BALMY DAYS sped by, each one prettier than the one before, wrapping up the end of June like a wedding gift and opening July like a flower. Emily's work at the Wild Rose began every morning at dawn and continued until after nightfall, when the tired laughter of familiar patrons drifted up to her open window from the taproom, and a gentle moon rose over Marblehead Harbor. Each day, Emily thought she would warn Lucy away from growing too attached to Moses, but somehow she never had the heart to do it nor ever found the right moment to try. She was busy, and Lucy was busy, and people came and went at the Wild Rose, asking for rooms, asking for meals, inquiring after musical events and lectures and charity picnics, and somehow the moment never came when Emily could take Lucy aside.

And every afternoon without fail, Emily took Blount out on the *Rosy*. By Saturday, it had come to seem that they had been sailing together forever. Sometimes he brought his sketchbook along, and Emily was becoming accustomed to being used as a model. But he always put the book aside eagerly when she gave him the helm.

"You're learning fast," she told him as he brought the little craft handily about.

"You're a very good teacher," Blount returned. "You seem to know everything."

She smiled happily and shook the hair out of her face as the wind shifted around her. Blount had the tiller and mainsheet, and Emily braced herself against the gunwale, watching him handle the boat and hearing the rush of wind past her ears. Blount had traded his city clothes for more practical canvas britches and a white linen shirt. His skin was growing bronzed from the wind and sun, and his brown hair was shot through with gold-colored strands. As Emily's gaze rested on him, Blount looked at her and gave her a smile that set her pulse racing. Her grip tightened on the gunwales.

"I think it's time to come about again," she said breathlessly, looking out at the water.

"I'd like to keep to this tack forever," Blount said. "Why can't we just sail out of the harbor and keep on going?"

"Because I'd miss my dinner," Emily replied, trying to sound light and careless. "And because tomorrow is Independence Day and we'd miss the fireworks, that's why."

"That was meant as a compliment."

"Oh, was it?" Emily said. She narrowed her eyes against the wind and thought wildly and foolishly that they could sail out of the harbor and keep going, that it was exactly what she had always wanted to do, and that if they did, Blount would say charming and flattering things to her by the hour, on and on without fail.

"I'd love to know what you're thinking," he said.

The color rushed to her cheeks. "I'm—I'm thinking about my dinner," she stammered. "And I wish I could have it."

She took the seat beside him and reached for the tiller, thinking he would give it up. But he did not let go, and her hand closed over his.

"Oh, I'm sorry," Emily said, pulling away.

"I'm not."

She knew he was looking at her, waiting for her to meet his eyes, but she was afraid to. He let go the tiller. The boat came about, the sail lost its wind, and they drifted, the sun suddenly hot and bright and still. He was not sketching her but still looking at her with an intensity that suggested he was memorizing her every feature. No one had ever looked at her that way before, and Emily felt light-headed with alarm and excitement and wonder, as though she were being hurled toward something she wasn't sure she wanted to reach. At last, Emily lifted her face and looked up at Blount. He shook his head slowly and smiled.

"You're just as sweet as can be," he whispered, tenderly pulling a strand of hair away from Emily's lips.

Emily turned away, her cheeks flaming. "No, I'm not. I'm as sour as a pickle, and it's time to go home," she said in confusion.

"If that's what you want," Blount said.

She swallowed hard. "It is," she lied, and steered the *Rosy* back to dock.

While she was tying up the boat, Blount put one hand on her arm. "I didn't mean to scare you," he said.

"My gracious, don't be silly," Emily replied, busy with the stern line. "I just have so much work to do, I don't know what makes me think I can spend all day sailing. As delightful as the company is," she added saucily.

"I reckon I have to be satisfied with that for now," Blount said. "But at least let me help you."

"No." Emily shook her head so hard her hair threatened to come completely loosened. "I have my own way of doing things and you'll only bother me. I wish you'd go."

Blount scratched his head in perplexity. "I'll see you later, then," he said.

"Unless you're leaving the Wild Rose, I guess you will."

Emily concentrated on the lines, busying herself with wildly erratic knots and trying to keep her hands from trembling. She heard the hollow wooden tread of Blount's footsteps on the dock. At last, she glanced over her shoulder, saw he was gone, and collapsed in a heap.

"Oh, my gracious," she whispered. Emily leaned over the edge of the pier and dipped her hand in the water to cool her forehead. She couldn't understand why her knees felt so weak whenever Blount smiled at her, and it alarmed her tremendously. He wasn't at all the sort of man she admired, all manners and graces and polish, looking as though he had just stepped out of a men's outfitters. She had been raised to respect the stalwarts of Marblehead, the grim-faced fishing folk, the sober black-coated ministers and schoolmasters, the no-nonsense Yankees who wrestled with God and the whale.

"Blount is entirely frivolous," she whispered to herself emphatically. "And he doesn't know how to make anything but pretty compliments."

Feeling steadier, Emily gathered herself up, finished securing the *Rosy,* and headed home. But before she reached Front Street she turned aside, knowing that she wasn't yet ready to risk meeting Blount again at home. She lingered for a moment in front of a dress-shop window, seeing her own face reflected back at her, hearing over and over again Blount's voice, sweet and warm, in her ear. She shivered.

The bell over the shop door tinkled and Lucy came out onto the step. She stopped dead when she saw Emily, and hastily put her hand behind her back.

"Lucy," Emily said with a smile.

"I was on my way to find you," Lucy replied.

"In the dress shop?"

"Maybe I should have looked at the tailor's."

Emily blushed. "I don't know what you mean."

"I don't know what's so charming about that boy, but every time I look around, you're with him," Lucy said as they fell into step on the sidewalk.

"I'm only teaching him to sail." Emily glanced sideways at her friend. "To show Micah I'm a good enough sailor to teach a landsman. I told you that."

"Mmmhmm."

"I don't see what's so terrible about it," Emily said.

"No, I guess you don't," Lucy answered without looking at her.

Emily frowned as she looked at Lucy's stubborn profile. "If it's because he's—his father owns—" She foundered on the words, casting about for the right thing to say. "He thinks you're as bright as a new penny."

"For a nigger?" Lucy asked sharply. "I'm flattered that he would condescend to patronize me."

"Lucy!"

Her friend sighed. "I guess I just wish you didn't find him such interesting company. That's all."

Emily scratched her elbow, itching with frustration, and searched for a way to turn the topic. She heard the rustle of paper in Lucy's hand.

"Well, what have you bought?" Emily asked.

"It isn't anything," Lucy replied.

"I don't believe it," Emily said. "I know you don't come out of the dress shop with a bag of air."

"Some people seem to know everything."

They both nodded to the deacon's wife as they passed her coming out of Mr. Ledue's dry-goods store. "It's only a yard of ribbon," Lucy explained.

"To make yourself look pretty for Moses?" Emily asked, stopping dead in her tracks. "Now Lucy, I want to tell you—"

"Tell me what?"

Emily faltered before Lucy's steady look. "Only that I'm worried about you," she admitted. "And I don't want to ever see you hurt."

Lucy looked away, squinting in the glare of the sun. "I know you don't."

There didn't seem to be anything else to say. Emily frowned as they continued up the lane and turned onto Front Street. Then they both halted. In front of the Wild Rose, Mr. Stockwell was trying to mount a hired bay horse. Moses was holding the horse's head, but it was sidestepping in a marish way and rolling its eyes as a piece of newspaper came billowing and scudding down the street. Mr. Stockwell lifted his foot to the stirrup but then fell heavily against the horse as it shifted.

"You damn idiot!" Mr. Stockwell shouted, raising his riding crop. He quirted Moses across the shoulders with it.

Emily gaped, speechless.

Lucy made a stifled sound, and Emily clutched Lucy's arm as her friend moved forward.

"No, don't," she warned.

In an instant, Lucy wrenched her arm away and turned on Emily. "Don't? Don't make trouble? Is that what you were going to say?"

"I—" Emily stared at her.

"That man would rather hit Moses than a horse, but he's our guest, isn't that it?" Lucy accused her. "For the sake of peace and good manners you'll stand by and watch that happen? You won't challenge him at all?"

Emily shook her head. She was stunned to hear such bitter words. "No, that's not what I meant."

"Then what?" Lucy demanded. Her voice rose. *"What?"*

"Lucy, hush!" Emily dragged her friend into an alley, out of sight of Mr. Stockwell. Lucy came grudgingly, dragging her feet and staring at the ground.

"Listen to me, Lucy," Emily said. "That was a low, despicable thing that Mr. Stockwell did, but you can't go rushing at him! What did you think you'd do?"

"Hit him, scratch his eyes out, something."

"Holy God!" Emily threw her hands up. "How can you think of such a thing? He'd have you arrested for assault and hauled off to court—or—or he'd turn you over to that skulking Mr. Pinkham and say you belonged to a neighbor of his."

Lucy drew an unsteady breath, glaring defiantly at Emily. Her eyes glittered.

"Lucy," Emily pleaded. "Lucy, please, I'm so afraid for you. There's nothing we can do to lighten Moses's load. He's a slave."

"Not for long," Lucy muttered.

Emily stared. "What?"

Lucy smoothed back her hair with a shaking hand and walked several steps down the alley. "He's going to run away," she said in a voice that shook as much as her hand did. "And I aim to help him."

"You *do*?" Emily squeaked.

"Yes, I do," Lucy said vehemently. "And if you're the person I believe you are, you'll help."

81

"Why, my gracious." Emily stared into space, at a loss for words. Then she shook herself. "Why, it'd be like a real adventure. It'd be famous!"

She smiled excitedly and grabbed Lucy's hands. "I think it's a wonderful idea!" she said. "You bet I'll help you; I wouldn't miss out for the world!"

"This ain't a prank I'm talking about," Lucy said, eying Emily askance. "This ain't like putting pepper in Mr. Ledue's snuffbox."

"Oh, that was just a silly thing I did when I was a child," Emily said with a dismissive wave of her hand. "Why, I already feel like the heroine in one of those penny dreadfuls."

Lucy looked down, her face troubled. "I wish you'd treat it more serious."

"Oh, I will, I do," Emily said with a quick nod. She breathed in deeply. The scent of hot dust, salt, and fish was suddenly sharper and more exciting than ever, and Emily felt a prickle of anticipation in her fingertips. Nearby, the clanking of a press from a print shop made a forward, dynamic sound like the rushing of train wheels. Emily tucked both hands through Lucy's arm. "Come on, let's go home."

"Home?" Lucy asked in a strange voice.

Emily shook her impatiently. "Yes, now, let's go. You see to Moses and tell him I'm on his side one hundred percent."

Without waiting for Lucy's reply, Emily raced back to the Wild Rose, kicking up her gingham skirt behind her. She entered the house through the garden, pausing in the shed off the kitchen to clean some horse manure off her shoe.

Her father's and sister's voices reached her, low and solemn, as she scuffed her shoe against a scraper. In the frame of mind Emily was in, their voices sounded like the voices of conspirators.

". . . was here today again," Mr. MacKenzie said.

Lavinia replied quickly. "For how long?"

"Not long," their father said. "He shouldn't be back here, not tonight, anyway, so we'll make out fine. But we'll have to make other arrangements."

Emily, standing on one foot, lost her balance and toppled into a stack of kindling, sending it tumbling to the floor with a crash.

Footsteps hurried across the kitchen floor, and Mr. MacKenzie appeared in the doorway, his face grim. Then he smiled.

"Oh, Emily."

"Hello, Father," Emily said, gathering the split wood into a hasty stack. "I knocked over the woodpile. Again."

"You've always been the clumsiest child I know," he said with a chuckle as he bent to help her.

"Father," Emily asked. "Who were you and Lavvy speaking of?"

"Oh, nobody that matters," he replied with an absent shake of his head. "It's nothing for you to worry about."

Emily felt a shiver of delight to think that her father and sister were concerned with such mundane matters, and for once, she felt a supercilious sense of importance when her father patted her on the cheek and left through the back door. He thought she was a child, and always treated her as one, but unbeknownst to him, she was poised on the brink of intrigue, peril, and suspense.

"Hello, Lavvy," Emily sang out as she entered the kitchen.

Lavinia was rolling piecrust. "Hello, Em," she answered, panting over her work. She paused to scrape off a bit of dough that was stuck to the whalebone rolling pin.

"Making a pie?" Emily asked.

Lavinia smiled tiredly and wiped her forehead with the back of her hand. "Cherry," she puffed. "Zachary's favorite."

"It's just too bad he ain't here to have some," Emily said, sitting down at the table. In front of her was a bowl of bright red sour cherries, their skins gleaming. Frowning, she picked one out and squeezed it until the stone popped out into her hand.

"If you'll get those pitted, I'd be glad," Lavinia said.

Emily nodded, and waved aside a fly that was exploring the rim of the bowl. She listened absently to the gentle thump-bump of the rolling pin as Lavinia pressed it down across the pastry. Her sister started in on a tale about their neighbor's eccentric dog, but Emily did not attend.

"Say, Lavvy," Emily broke in. "You know that fellow, Mr. Pinkham?"

The rolling pin jerked in Lavvy's hands. "What makes you ask about a man like him?"

Emily squeezed the stone out of another cherry and ate the fruit. "He said there's a gang of abolitionists around here that smuggle slaves. Who do you suppose he meant? Could it be anyone in the Anti-Slavery Society?"

"I can't imagine," Lavinia said. She drew a deep breath and took a sip of cool water from a glass. Her hand trembled.

Emily felt a pang of anxiety. "You look awful tired, Lavvy."

"No, I'm fine, I'm fine," Lavinia said.

As her sister continued rolling the piecrust, Emily wondered to herself if she had been a bit hasty, as usual. Although her attention to politics and laws was fleeting at best, she did know that helping a slave to run away was a crime. For weeks, the tavern had resounded with hot debate over the Dred Scott decision, which had ruled slaves to be the private property of the slave owner. The result was that abetting a runaway meant stealing. It made no difference to the law if the state where the theft occurred was free or slave: theft was theft, and the courts were strict.

Emily plucked another handful of cherries from the bowl, her hands sticky with sour juice, and glanced at Lavinia from under her lashes. The last thing her sister needed at the moment was for Emily to get into trouble with the law, Emily realized with chagrin. For once, it behooved her to think of something other than the potential for adventure and her own enjoyment of it. Emily dreaded being the cause of any pain to Lavinia, and judging by her own experience, she was likely to fling herself headfirst into a mess and do precisely that.

"Oh!" Emily yelped, pushing herself abruptly away from the table.

Lavinia looked up in surprise. "Did you bite your tongue?"

"I've got to find Lucy," Emily said, and rushed out of the kitchen.

# Chapter Seven

HER FOOTSTEPS ECHOED loudly in the hallway as she raced through the inn, slamming open doors and looking into the taproom. Lucy was nowhere to be found. With growing frustration, Emily ran back toward the kitchen to the hidden passageway and put her shoulder to the panel. She rebounded with a tooth-jarring thud.

"Why, whatever's the matter?" she moaned, blinking in annoyance.

She pounded on the panel. "Oh, I'm in a hurry," she muttered. "Why is this stuck? What is wrong with this thing? Is there somebody there?" she asked as a faint sound reached her ear. She pounded again on the door.

There was a gasp behind her. "What are you doing?" Lavinia asked.

Emily turned. The noise had drawn Lavinia from the kitchen, and now her sister stood with one hand on the door frame, pale and staring. Emily gaped at her.

"What are you doing?" Lavinia repeated sharply.

"I wanted to take the shortcut," Emily said, puzzled by her sister's tone. "It sounds as though someone might be in there and I—"

Lavinia came forward with surprising swiftness and took Emily's arm. "You're making enough noise to wake the dead," she said. "If the door is stuck, you'll just have to go around. And when you're through racing around the house, you can finish those cherries and then sweep the floor in the taproom." With a none-too-gentle shove, she sent Emily back down the hallway.

Baffled and hurt, Emily went as Lavinia bade her, casting one glance over her shoulder. Lavinia was standing by the secret panel, watching Emily with her arms folded above her belly.

"I'm going," Emily said. "Don't you worry about me."

Lavinia relaxed somewhat. "I won't."

Emily shrugged. The emotional vagaries of pregnant women were well known, and it was her duty to indulge and protect Lavinia if she could. With a sick turning beneath her ribs, Emily remembered what she had made up her mind to do. She plodded reluctantly up the stairs.

The corridor stretched away on either side before turning a corner at each end. A mellow light slanted through one open window onto the plank floor, and with it came the sound of a fiddle being played in another house. Emily heard a low murmur from behind the door of Mrs. Stockwell's room, a gentle voice she knew to be

Blount's, and a faint, nearly inaudible whining in response.

It struck Emily as bizarre and pathetic that a disposition as sunny as Blount's should be wasted on such a mother—and his father. She almost wished she did dare help Moses run away, if only to vex them. But no, she decided. She had to consider Lavinia.

"Lucy?" she said softly, entering an empty guest room whose door stood open.

Lucy was cleaning the windows so vigorously, Emily was afraid the old panes would crack. A bowl of vinegar gave off pungent fumes from the dresser, and a pile of damp and crumpled newspapers on the painted floor cloth proved that Lucy had been hard at work.

"I have to tell you something," Emily said, closing the door carefully behind her.

Lucy nodded, still wiping the glass with swift, hard strokes. "Go on."

Emily paused, hating to disappoint her friend but feeling a solemn sense of duty toward Lavinia. She also felt a creeping nervousness that the Stockwells were so close by.

"Lucy," she whispered. "What I said I'd do before . . . Well, I don't believe I can do it, after all."

Instantly, Lucy went still. She did not speak or turn around. Emily felt her skin flush all over.

"It's too risky," she hurried on. "I know you think I'm being selfish, but this is your home too, and Lavinia's been like a mother to both of us and she's just ready to drop, and she's missing Zachary so much, and I just don't think we should get into any kind of trouble. Don't you see?" she rushed on desperately when Lucy still didn't move. "Please say something!"

At last, Lucy turned around. Her face was without expression and she looked not at Emily but at the blank, papered wall behind her. "You are not going to help," she said in a flat voice.

"No, I just think it's a terribly unwise thing to do," Emily insisted, taking an urgent step forward. "And I don't think you should get involved in this, either."

Lucy's gaze moved to Emily's face. She began to shake her head slowly back and forth. "You are not the person I thought you were," she said coldly.

Emily felt a jolt run through her. "Why, Lucy," she whispered, "you don't mean that. You know I only want to do what's right. I swear, I've given this a great deal of thought."

"You never gave a great deal of thought to anything in your life," Lucy flung back at her. "But, for once, maybe you ought to do so."

While Emily stood dumbstruck in the middle of the room, Lucy methodically gathered her cleaning supplies together and left. Emily stared out the window, feeling lower than she'd ever felt in her life.

"I am such a fool," she whispered. "Such a fool."

She stood there for another long moment, and then turned and walked slowly out into the hallway. Emily paused by the window and stared out at the blue sky. Behind her, a door opened and shut.

"Emily? Miss MacKenzie?"

Emily flinched at the sound of Blount's voice.

"Yes?" she faltered.

She heard his footsteps behind her, and when she was confident that her face would not somehow betray Lucy's scheme, she looked up at him. Blount's expression was sorrowful.

"What is it?" she asked.

"My parents have decided to remove from here," he replied in a dejected tone. "I'm sorry. It is no reflection on you or your family, but my mother complains of the noise and some factors which to her are great inconveniences."

Emily looked away, feeling a bitter darkness in her heart. "Are you removing to the Ship?"

"Yes. That is the name of the place we're going to." Blount sighed. "Can we walk out for a moment? I would like to speak with you."

Emily felt a growing, irrational rage against Micah Handy. His family had always thwarted hers. She was sure he had conspired to lure the Stockwells away, and even though she had grown tired of Mr. and Mrs. Stockwell's petty grievances, she knew the Wild Rose would miss their patronage. She knew also that Lucy would be stricken to know Moses was leaving the house; but with Moses elsewhere in Marblehead, Lavinia would not be implicated in any scheme of his to run away. Emily's head swam.

"I'll walk out with you," she said tiredly.

Without speaking, they went single file down the narrow staircase, through the quiet tavern and out into the street.

A confused gabble of shouts suddenly filled the streets.

"Runaway!"

Emily felt her heart skip a beat. "No!" she gasped. "Not now!"

"Emily?" Blount said.

Then a riderless horse came galloping around the corner, reins dangling, stirrups bouncing, mane flying. A crowd of men chased after it, and horse and men all disappeared down an alley. A thin cloud of dust bowled down the street after them.

"Oh, dear God," Emily breathed.

"There, don't worry," Blount said, taking her arm. He smiled at her. "You looked terrified. I guess you're not quite as fearless as you always seem to be."

"No, I mean yes," Emily said quickly, realizing it was best to let him think she was afraid of horses. "Last summer we had an exposition and a parade with elephants, and the horses all went off their heads. It's the smell of the elephants that scares them, you see, and there was quite a stampede and I was almost trampled, and I even lost my hat," she rushed on, improvising wildly as she went.

Blount nodded. "I understand. Now, I wanted to tell you something," he said, carefully plucking a bit of floating dandelion fluff from the air. He held it in his hand, and then blew it off. "We're moving to another establishment, but I hope I can still . . ."

He trailed off, and gave her an earnest, hopeful smile.

"Oh, of course," Emily said as she took his meaning. "That is, this is a public house, and anyone can visit, although you'll find the patrons at the Ship more elegant than we are," she said with some bitterness.

"I don't think I will," Blount told her. "Your family is the most loving I've known, and your house the most welcoming."

Their eyes met and a silence came between them. Emily broke away and walked beside the fence, pausing to look at the roses as a peculiar confusion of emotions ran through her heart. She was very sorry to see Blount go, glad that he preferred not to; she was happy to be rid of his parents, but jealous that they had chosen the Handys'; and she was relieved to know Moses would be somewhere else, for his removal meant the removal of barriers between her and Lucy.

But mostly, when she looked at Blount again, she felt like smiling.

"Emily!" Lavinia's voice came from the house.

"My sister needs me," Emily said breathlessly. "Good-bye."

"No, not good-bye," Blount replied. "Until next time."

Emily nodded, and hurried through the gate.

That night, Emily slipped into the noisy taproom and stood by the door to scan the crowd. Nearby, a doleful itinerant silhouette cutter who was putting up at the inn sat snipping away at a piece of black paper.

Across from him, Mr. Ledue sat in profile, his sharp nose aquiver with curiosity. He was trying to see out of the corner of his eye how his portrait was coming along. Ham Holliwell sat at the silhouette cutter's shoulder, puffing his pipe and snorting from time to time.

"How does it look to you, Emily?" Mr. Ledue asked.

"Oh, just fine," Emily said, frowning as she looked at the man's profile rendered in black. She wondered if there was an etiquette she didn't understand, which dictated that white faces must be silhouetted in black, and black faces in white. Then she tried to think if she had ever seen a silhouette cutter offer to portray a black person, and realized she never had.

Leaving her post by the door, Emily threaded her way between the tables to sit down across from Mr. Polk.

"Well, good evening to you, Emily," the minister said, putting down his newspaper with a friendly nod.

"Good evening, sir," she replied. She scooted her chair closer to his. "I am glad to find you alone, Mr. Polk, as I have something quite serious to consult with you about."

"Oh, do you?" the man said, smiling indulgently. "If it's to be excused from church tomorrow if the weather's fine for sailing, I'll have to say no. Just because it'll be the Fourth of July doesn't give you independence from the Sabbath."

Emily shook her head. "No, not this time. It's about . . ." She looked around swiftly and lowered her voice. "Abolition. And the Anti-Slavery Society."

"Yes?" he prompted her. He took off his spectacles

and frowned at them, and then his eyes sought Emily's father at the bar. Mr. MacKenzie met his gaze and then looked away. "What is it you wish to know, Emily?" the minister asked quietly.

Emily clasped her hands together in her lap to keep them from betraying her excitement. "What happens when a slave runs away?" she asked.

Mr. Polk's head snapped up at her question. He looked at her acutely. "What makes you ask that?"

"I'm curious," she said, anxious to put things right between her and Lucy, and keeping a curb on her tongue, for once.

He exhaled slowly through his nose, and then carefully fitted his spectacles back on. "Let us take a suppositious case," Mr. Polk began. "Let us say that a slave arrives in Marblehead, openly or otherwise."

"Yes," Emily said eagerly.

"There might be found certain people who would be willing to hide that person for some period of time." Mr. Polk's gaze again wandered around the room before returning to Emily. "Do you understand me?"

"I think so," Emily said. "Then what happens?"

"As I say, these hypothetical people might be willing to hide such a person for some period of time until a ship bound for Nova Scotia or another part of Canada can be found to convey him there."

Emily's heart began to trip with excitement. Her imagination filled with the creaking of hawsers, the quiet dip and pull of oars in a black nighttime ocean. She longed to take part in adventure so much she felt giddy.

"Mr. Polk," she said, putting one hand on his arm. "Who are these people?"

Mr. Polk rested his hand on his folded newspaper and traced a line of type with one bony finger. "These people are entirely supposititious and hypothetical," he said, and then added with quiet emphasis, "as supposititious as the slave in the case we speak of."

Emily took her hand away from his arm. "I think I know what you mean to tell me," she said hesitantly. "If there's no *actual* slave, there are no actual people to help him."

The minister was silent, frowning at his paper. The noise of the tavern flowed over and around them in waves, and a sudden burst of laughter by the silhouette cutter made Emily jump in her chair.

"Am I right?" she whispered, her eyes bright.

Mr. Polk looked up at her with a swift, kindly smile. "I'll see you in church tomorrow morning, come rain or shine, won't I?"

Emily gave him a crooked smile. "Very well. I won't ask anything else. You will see me tomorrow, sir. Thank you for your advice."

"Good night, Emily."

She stood up from the table, wondering what to do with her new information. So much had happened during the day that her head was swimming. Emily said good night, and then went to her room.

# *Chapter Eight*

EMILY'S DREAMS WERE filled with bizarre phantoms made from the preoccupations of her day. There were urgent whispers, soft footfalls, and the stealthy closing of doors; she dreamed she heard Lavinia's voice and her father's and even Micah's. Emily tossed in her sleep, seeing dark figures slip between shadow and shadow, knowing that these were runaway slaves she was dreaming of but not knowing if she should help, powerless to help no matter what she wished. Lavinia was there, and she knew she must keep Lavinia from harm, but then Mr. Polk told her that these slaves were supposititious and hypothetical, and Emily's anxiety passed into vague and formless dreams that faded into nothing at the Sunday sunrise.

And although Lucy was quiet and withdrawn, and reserved in her manner toward Emily as they went to church, Emily was convinced that she could find a way to heal the breach between them. The solemn and majestic words of Mr. Polk's Independence Day sermon fell on her ears; the morning light streamed through the eastern windows in golden bars; the murmurous voice of the wind and distant surf filled the church like the whispering voice of God to such a degree that Emily was at last convinced of her own capability and the straightness of her vision.

"Don't you worry," she whispered to Lucy. She took Lucy's hand in hers and gave it a warm squeeze. The organ began wheezing and the congregation rose for a hymn.

Lucy looked at her sideways as she stood. "What are you talking about?" she whispered back.

Emily felt a catch in her throat as the familiar opening chords of "A Mighty Fortress Is Our God" filled the church. She was sure there was a way for Moses to gain his freedom and for Lucy's confidence in her to be restored. Solutions were always available, and new courses could be charted to meet the changing wind and tides. It was a more challenging course, but she could meet it.

As Emily opened her mouth to sing, her gaze lit upon a man hurrying up the side aisle and bending to speak to another man at the end of the pew ahead of her. When the man in the pew turned his head, she recognized Mr. Pinkham, the bounty hunter. Emily's mouth went dry.

The congregation began to sing, and Lucy and Lavinia sang on either side of Emily, their alto voices strong and resolute and clear. But a wave of uncertainty pooled ominously around Emily's heart. If Lucy were caught giving aid to a runaway, what would her position be? As the descendant of slaves, however remote, to what convoluted laws was Lucy subject and what evil retribution might befall her?

Emily looked fearfully from Lucy to the bounty hunter. The seams, collar, and cuffs of his coat were shiny with age, and there was a grime of dirt on the back of his neck. He was loathsome, and his appearance seemed the outward promise that he had neither pity nor mercy. For days he had been walking about town, engaging anyone he could in conversation, sniffing around for clandestine activity. Now, as he left with his companion, Emily felt her stomach sink.

With round, fearful eyes, she looked back at Lucy, seeing Lucy's throat move up and down with her singing, seeing the shadow of her lashes on her cheek as she read from the hymnal, her hair and her thin shoulders; in Emily's ear sounded the voice she had fallen asleep to on so many nights.

Emily felt sick.

"What is wrong with you?" Lucy asked under the chorus of the hymn.

Emily shook her head, her eyes swimming with tears. The thought of Lucy being remanded into slavery made her want to weep; the thought of Lucy being taken from her as suddenly and irrevocably as her own mother threw her into a well of desolation, and she hung her head.

The voice of the congregation swelled in the final "Amen," and Emily sank into her seat.

"Are you feeling faint?" Lavinia whispered, leaning close.

Emily shook her head silently.

"Then what's come over you?"

Emily raised her eyes bleakly to her sister's face. "Why did our mother have to die?" she whispered.

"Oh, pet," Lavinia sighed, slipping her arm around Emily's shoulders.

Emily rested her head against Lavinia, trying not to ask herself which would be worse, risking Lucy or letting the Stockwells know that Moses was planning his escape.

At the end of the service, Emily trailed out of the church, hardly returning the Sabbath greetings of her neighbors. She stepped out onto the porch, blinking for a moment in the sunlight as her family went on ahead of her down the steps.

"You look as peaked as a consumptive," declared Granny Godwin, fingering the edge of Emily's shawl.

Emily stopped and looked down into a pair of bright, snapping eyes framed by a black bonnet. "I'm a little tired," she said.

"Tired? I don't believe it! Young people do nothing but sleep!" Granny Godwin tipped her head to one side like a bird, her lips working in and out over her toothless gums. "Isn't that so?" she demanded in a loud and penetrating voice.

"Why—I—" Emily stammered, looking desperately around the crowd for an excuse to break away. Micah, standing on a lower step, looked up and made as though to move toward her.

"Never knew you to be nervous, though you take after your mother, and of course your mother was nervous, God rest her soul," the old woman continued with obvious relish at surviving for so long. "Too young to die was that one."

Emily felt a lump in her throat. "Yes, she was."

"Never should have nursed Lucy's parents, I always said, and didn't she take the scarlatina from them? She was well in the morning and died that night. They were decent God-fearing folk but should have found some of their own people to nurse them."

"Granny Godwin!" Micah broke in. He came forward with a brilliant smile for the old lady and took her arm to lead her away. "You look as bright as a daisy today."

"Wicked flatterer!" Granny snapped, her eyes bright.

Over the heads of the chatting churchgoers, Emily spied Blount waiting with his hat in hand and a basket covered by a napkin in the other. She knew he was waiting for her, and she wanted nothing else so much as to walk away with him, away from Lucy's silent expectations, away from her own duty to Lavinia, away from the anger and despair that were growing in her.

"I see someone I meant to speak to," she choked out. "Good-bye, Granny."

Micah bit back a reply as Emily slipped through the homeward streaming crowd and struggled to fight clear of the current. At last she emerged breathlessly on the far side and landed almost at Blount's feet. His smile widened.

"Hello," she said, catching her breath.

"Now I know why we go to the Methodist church," Blount said. "It's so I could be here waiting for you when your service let out."

Emily sighed. She had little heart for his compliments yet. "I'll admit I am glad to see you," she told him as she tucked her psalm book into her pocket. "Granny Godwin was making me feel pretty low."

"I'm pleased I could come to your rescue, then." They fell into step together, and Blount offered her his arm. "I'm sorry you feel sad. Has something happened?"

She shook her head, feeling the impossibility of telling him the truth. Her thoughts were terribly mixed, but she was sensible enough to know that she mustn't let on an inkling to Blount of what had put her in such a quandary.

And he seemed content to walk with her silently, allowing her some time for reflection. Their way took them up the sloping path of Burial Hill. Emily felt the cool air lift the curls from the back of her neck, and heard quiet bird song from a crab apple tree. It was peaceful and restful. Emily was glad to walk at Blount's side through the springy, rock-studded grass.

But the absurdity of the situation was not lost on her. She was contemplating the abduction of his family's property, although to think of Moses as property went against her Yankee nature. To carry through the plan meant to commit a crime against Blount, who had been kind to her and respectful to Lucy. She felt an uncomfortable sense of treachery and guilt, accepting—even en-

102

couraging—his attentions and compliments when she was secretly scheming to harm him.

But for Lucy's sake, and Lavinia's, she remembered, she was more than halfway determined not to carry through the plan. And so there was no reason for guilt at all. She could welcome his friendship without reserve.

Emily stopped on the track and raised her eyes to look around her. Blount paused, not speaking, graciously offering his silence until she felt able to speak. She watched him wander tactfully away, intent on the scattered grave markers.

"This is where many of my ancestors are buried," Emily said, meandering among the headstones after him. The sun rested its warm arms across her shoulders like an old friend, and familiar names called to her from either side: Penworthy, Carter, Muir, Bull. And at every turn, there was a MacKenzie, some lost at sea, some carried away in infancy or childbirth, some killed in battle, some rare few dead of old age.

"Was this the smuggler you told me about?" Blount asked from nearby. He bent to a lichen-covered stone, frowning over the carved inscription under a rampant eagle. "It says Lieutenant John MacKenzie."

"Yes, that's him." Emily joined him and pointed to other stones. "And there, his father and mother, and his sister, Ann, and her husband. And look here," she added.

Emily knelt in the warm, scented grass before a stone so worn by time that its words had almost vanished. She traced the letters with one finger. "Here lies Ian MacKenzie, also Flora, beloved wife and mother."

She pressed her hand flat against the stone. It was rough but warm, as though the blood of the entire family beat within it.

"They were the first of my clan to reach these shores, and built our house. They must have been so brave," Emily said, her voice gruff. "The winters here are so fierce, and it so easy to sicken and die."

She heard Blount's tread behind her and knew that if she leaned back, she would rest against him. Her heart ached.

"Is your mother here?" he asked tenderly.

Tears sprang to Emily's eyes. She blinked them away quickly and nodded. With a sigh, Blount lowered himself to the grass beside her and sat back against another MacKenzie's stone. His face was thoughtful, and he toyed with the handle of the basket he carried.

"You must have loved her very much to miss her still," he said.

Emily nodded, but didn't choose to look toward her mother's grave. She gazed mournfully at Ian and Flora's marker.

"I think I know what you feel," Blount said quietly. "I miss my mother, too."

"But she's alive." Emily brushed away a tear as she looked at him.

Blount shrugged, and looked out over the treetops of the town below. On the water, sleek yachts beat toward the harbor's mouth, leaning out keenly over the waves.

"When I was very young, my mother was like a robin," Blount began. "She sang all day long, was always busy going here and there, always visiting the sick and the poor, making things for missionaries, having musical evenings. She had a wide acquaintance and would read us the news in her friends' letters from Baltimore and Washington and Charlotte."

Emily stared. The wan, dreary woman she knew as Mrs. Stockwell was nothing like he described. "But what happened to change her?" she blurted out.

Blount shook his head, and a painful blush spread across his face. "I believe I know, but it is not polite to mention," he said.

"Please, you can confide in me," Emily pressed him.

Blount winced. "My father—there was a girl in our house who worked in the kitchen. She was Moses's sister. I was only ten, but I believe . . ."

"Your father made one of your slaves his mistress?"

"I'm not certain." Blount sighed. "But she was sold away, and my mother changed. I believe that was the reason."

Emily put one hand on his arm. "Have you asked her?"

"No, no," he said, giving her a pained smile. "I couldn't. She'd only give me that frightened-rabbit look and change the subject."

"And was that also why you and Moses ended your friendship?"

Blount nodded, brooding over his own well-hidden sorrows and regrets. Emily plucked at the grass by her side, surprised to find someone so outwardly carefree had nursed such a sadness on his own. She wanted to hold his hand and tell him she understood, that she was power-fully moved by his reticence, and honored him for it. A grasshopper bounded onto the sleeve of his coat, and she picked it off carefully.

"Blount, I'd like to apologize to you," she said, choosing her words slowly and keeping her eyes on the grasshopper in her hands. "I believe I judged you wrongly at first."

"You don't need to—"

"No, please," she broke in. She could feel the grass-hopper's tiny legs move against her palms. "I know I'm not an idiot, but neither am I a deep thinker. I just don't consider things very much. And so I want to say that I'm sorry if at first I judged you wicked because of your fa-ther's slaves, and thought you a frivolous, careless person just because you dress like such a dandy and talk like an actor in a melodrama."

Blount laughed, and Emily looked up at him swiftly, her cheeks burning.

"I didn't mean any offense."

"I know you didn't," Blount said, smiling warmly. He turned her hands over to reveal the grasshopper. "Let it go."

Cautiously, she opened her hands, and the grasshop-per leaped away so quickly it seemed to disappear into the sunlight. Emily laughed from the surprise, and a sud-den gust of wind tossed her shawl off her shoulders. Her heart lifted.

"Things occur very fast in this world," Blount said, taking her hand and twining his fingers with hers. "In the blink of an eye a person might disappear forever or fall in love."

"Oh," Emily whispered, meeting his steady gaze with shy astonishment.

Blount raised her hand and pressed his lips to her open palm. Emily's blood seemed to halt in its course and then rocketed wildly. With his head still lowered over her hand, he murmured, "I have felt so much alone lately, but I never do when I am with you."

Emily's heart went out to him and to the entreaty in his voice. She looked down at his hair and wanted to kiss it. But some misgiving kept her from doing so, and at last she drew her hand away from him.

"Some people might fall in love quickly, but I don't know if I do," she said with difficulty. "I know I judged you too fast, but I do know we're different."

He straightened up. "No. Not so different as you think," he said.

If Emily looked into his eyes, she felt herself losing her train of thought, and so in some confusion, she stood up and walked out onto a rock ledge. The wind whipped her skirts against her legs. She squinted against the wind, watching the sloops and schooners plying the water far out to sea.

"I don't know how to explain this," she said, frowning hard as she tried to form her thoughts. Blount stood beside her, the breeze blowing his hair back from his forehead.

Emily forced herself to keep looking out at the ships. "I never have cared for politics. But I do feel that I am a

Yankee and you are a Southerner. And I feel that there is a deep core of difference there, although I can't say what it is."

"Are we back to the whaling ship metaphors?" Blount asked.

She shook her head with impatience. "I don't pay much attention to this question of states' rights, and I'm not sure how I feel about that. But I do know that we up here don't hold with slavery, and you do, even though it makes you sad and you don't behave unkindly."

Finally Emily looked at him, hoping to read some convincing denial in his face or some sign that he agreed with her and wished to give up his birthright. But instead, Blount gave her a quizzical look from under his arched brows.

"So you mean that you Yankees made your fortunes with your own labor and toil, and were graced by God's approval," he said.

Emily blushed, but raised her chin. "Yes, that's right," she said.

"And those fortunes," Blount went on musingly. He waved one hand seaward, where the richly trimmed yachts dared the Atlantic as proudly as kings and queens. "Those fortunes were made in shipping and trade. The merchant bankers of Boston, those hardy souls who braved the oceans."

"Yes," Emily said, growing puzzled and uncertain at his tone. She did not know where he was leading. "I have two older brothers in a shipping house in Boston. Massachusetts has relied on the sea for two hundred years and on its own sons and daughters."

"And not on the sons and daughters of Africa?" Blount asked.

Emily frowned. "No, you know it as well as I do."

Blount took her arm and turned her to face him. "Emily," he said. "Emily, what do you think they carried in those ships?"

"Why—timber and salt cod—and—" Emily cast about, battling a worrisome certainty that she was straying near hidden rocks. "And manufactured furnishings from Europe and—"

"And African captives," Blount said, folding his arms across his chest. "Molasses, rum, slaves. That is the unholy triangle that made those fortunes, Emily, the same fortunes that are now entertaining themselves on those beautiful sailboats out there."

Emily looked dumbly at the distant yachts and shook her head.

"They were Yankee ships that brought the slaves to us," Blount said gently. "It's clear to me that this is a fact you Yankees have managed to forget."

"I didn't know," Emily whispered. "No one ever told me."

"Your great-grandfather, the one who rowed for General Washington—didn't you say he smuggled rum and molasses?" Blount pressed on.

Emily nodded, and slowly sat down on the rock. The full green tops of the trees below waved like water, and birds darted among the moving branches like fish. Her rock ledge was like a boat with no tiller, and she did not know where she was going. "It was to help the family," she said haltingly. "And to confound the British."

"That molasses likely came off a ship from Barbados and filled the space vacated by African cargo," Blount said.

Emily tucked her knees up to her chin and rested her forehead against them.

"I don't mean to scold you or make you feel unhappy," Blount said, kneeling down beside her. "I only want to show you that things are not always what they seem to be or what we want them to be. I wish our system of agriculture did not rely on slavery, but it does. You believe Massachusetts has always been blameless and on the side of right, but it has not. Let's only be honest with ourselves, Emily. That is all I want."

Emily looked out at the harbor, amazed that the things she had always believed were not so at all. "We're all hypocrites, then?" she asked, bewildered and sad.

"Not you, Emily. Never you." Blount's voice was warm with tenderness.

"I—I don't know what to think anymore," Emily murmured. "Or what to do."

"Have a picnic with me, then," Blount suggested with a faint trace of his mischievous grin. He indicated the basket. "I brought grapes and sugar cakes. Now that I've left the Wild Rose, I can bring you a meal instead of the other way around, seeing it's the Fourth of July and all."

"Oh, Blount." Emily let out a sigh and smiled up at him. "You're so kind to me, and I don't know why."

"You don't?"

A blush swept across Emily's cheeks and she looked down into her lap, twisting her hands together. "Well, I guess I do."

"Then stay and have this picnic," he urged.

One of the churches in town began tolling its bell, and Emily felt her world return to her as instantly as the wind could shift on the water. "No, I should go home," she said reluctantly. "Sunday is a busy day for us and holidays, too, so I'll have too much work to do."

Blount watched her rise and made no effort to stop her. "Someday I hope you'll say yes."

"Perhaps I will," Emily told him.

"Will you be watching the fireworks tonight?" he asked.

"I'd like to," she admitted. "If I have time."

"Say you'll watch them with me."

Emily smiled shyly. "I will try to. I can promise I'll try."

"I'll have to settle for that, then," Blount said.

Still smiling, Emily turned and made her way back down the path. The bell continued tolling, and she was distantly aware of people shouting and a general movement of pedestrians up ahead toward one spot. Emily quickened her step and hurried into town.

"What is it?" she asked as a little boy ran by. "Is someone starting fireworks already?"

"I don't know, but I aim to go see!" he cried, one hand on his hat as he sped onward.

Emily followed the crowd down an alley, jostling amongst townfolk of all races and ages. Outside one of the old ropewalks, the thickest part of the crowd had gathered, and a desolate wailing rose above the noise of their voices. Emily edged her way through to the front, puzzled.

On hands and knees before the doorway was a black man in tattered clothes, blood oozing from a welt on the side of his head. Beside him stood a black woman in a ripped dress. It was she who was wailing, a high, inhuman sound, with her eyes open and staring at the crowd. Emily gaped at them in astonishment, and then noticed the irons on their legs and wrists.

"Out of the way," a gruff voice said. From behind them moved the bounty hunter, a smug look of satisfaction on his face.

"Runaways," someone in the crowd murmured. "The poor wretches."

"Must've been hiding in there, awaiting a ship," added someone else.

Two black men, brothers who ran a clam house on Gregory Street, stood with bowed heads, their hands clenched into fists at their sides, while their wives comforted their bewildered children. Mrs. Polk tried to aid the captive man, but Mr. Pinkham held her off with one arm.

"Sorry, ma'am," he said curtly. "I'll be obliged if you'd stand back."

"God forgive you," Mrs. Polk quavered as the slave woman continued to wail.

"Pitiful, but what can you do?" a man in the crowd murmured. "They knew the risk when they decided to cut and run, I guess."

"None of my business," another voice muttered. "The law's on his side."

"That's a mighty wicked law, then."

Emily stared, and as she did so, the captured woman turned and locked eyes with her. Emily heard a ringing in her ears and felt a gaping bleakness stretch wide inside her own heart.

"Help us," the woman begged.

Speechless, Emily held out her empty hands. "I can't."

"Please! Help us!" the woman sobbed again, staring beyond Emily. Mr. Pinkham pulled the woman backward, and someone in the crowd began muttering the Lord's Prayer.

"Emily, come away."

Someone took her arm. In a daze, Emily looked up into her father's face. He stood just behind her, his eyes filled with tears.

"Come away," he repeated gruffly. "There's nothing more we can do."

Emily followed him blindly, and as she stumbled through the crowd, she began to shiver. She feared she would never be able to erase those faces from her memory.

# Chapter Nine

AFTERNOON TRADE WAS brisk when Emily returned to the Wild Rose Inn, but she had no heart for her work. Even as she poured beer and served Sunday supper at six o'clock in the dining room, she did it as though in a mechanical stupor. Whenever her eyes rested on a blank surface, the wall, the floor, the table-cloth, her imagination painted the faces of the captured slaves upon it. Emily continually paused in her work, as though listening for something outside. Mr. Beady, the traveling silhouette cutter, had to speak to her twice before she heard him.

"Missy, is they any more baked beans?" he asked, giving his knife a good lick.

"I'll see," Emily replied, and then stood looking out the window at the garden. The lowering sun cast long shadows across the plot.

"That's not where you keep the beans, is it?" A widower, Dr. Broadbent, let out a roar of laughter and mashed lustily at his remaining beans with the back of his fork. "We don't want 'em fresh from the garden, Emily! I like mine with a little salt pork and molasses, if you please!" He guffawed again, and slapped the table with his broad palm.

Blushing, Emily hurried out of the dining room. Through the corridor to the kitchen, she passed the evidence of generations of MacKenzies: on curio shelves were heathen carvings from the South Seas, soot-darkened scrimshaw, a peculiar cup made from the eyeball of a whale, an old pistol, a stuffed crested bird; on the walls were sea charts and portraits on board, a framed sampler poorly stitched by Ann MacKenzie, daguerreotypes in faded velvet frames, and a colored etching of General Washington.

Prosperity and lean times had fluctuated like the tides in Marblehead, but through it all, the MacKenzies had found haven and refuge in the Wild Rose Inn, their own masters in their own dominion. Emily had seldom, if ever, given that freedom much consideration, but now it weighed heavily on her. As Emily walked into the kitchen, she wondered where the runaways would sleep that night.

Lavinia was sitting at the table, her head bowed over her clasped hands. Her lips moved silently, and Emily watched her pray.

"Amen," Lavinia whispered. She raised her head and looked at Emily with red-rimmed eyes.

"Were you praying for those slaves that got captured?" Emily asked.

Lavinia sniffed and drew a shaky breath. "I hope you will, too, Em. But now go on out. If you want to see the fireworks, you'll want a good prospect on the Neck. I can't tolerate a crowd tonight, so I'll mind things here."

"No," Emily said slowly, thinking of her promise to Blount. "I don't think I will go after all."

She replenished a serving dish with baked beans and carried it back to the dining room. Most of the guests had already excused themselves, leaving the Wild Rose unusually quiet.

"Ah, that's first-rate," Mr. Beady said, greedily watching Emily set the dish down among the soiled dishes and crumpled napery at his elbows.

"The fireworks will begin as soon as it's dark," Emily told him in a subdued tone. "You'll want to go find a good lookout."

Laughter and voices reached them through the open window, in a general movement of sound toward Marblehead Neck and the prospects of the harbor from its narrow, sandy spit.

The silhouette cutter shook his head. He spooned a heaping portion of baked beans onto his plate and garnished it with a dollop of corn relish from a cut-glass dish. "Such pyrotechnics hold no charms for me, young lady. I'll suit myself just fine in your father's tavern, and drink a toast to our Founding Fathers without the benefit of crackers blasting in my ears." He let out a dry chuckle.

"What toast will you raise to them?" Emily asked.

His lugubrious countenance was suddenly transformed with a smile. "Why, I'll drink to independence,

116

deliverance from tyranny, to the triumph of America's righteousness by the grace of God."

Emily felt his self-satisfied tone echo hollowly deep within her. He sounded alarmingly like herself. She turned and fled the room, burst into the kitchen, slammed the door shut behind her, and stood with her back against it.

"Why, whatever got into you?" Lavinia asked.

"A bilious attack of hypocrisy," Emily muttered.

Lavinia looked at her doubtfully and poured out a glass of buttermilk. "I never knew you to be subject to that before, Em." .

"I never was," Emily replied, sitting down at the table and propping her chin up in her hands. She scowled down at the tabletop, scarred and scorched by decades of knives and hot pans.

"Lavinia," she began, glancing up at her sister. "You know I am no philosopher, so you must help me think this through."

"I will."

Emily took a deep breath. Behind her, the door opened and Mr. MacKenzie came into the kitchen for supper.

"Our great-grandfather disobeyed the law when he was a smuggler, didn't he?" Emily asked, including Mr. MacKenzie in the question.

Their father looked startled. "Yes, that's true, he surely did," he said, setting down his dinner plate on the table and drawing out a chair.

"And it was right that he disobeyed the law, because

117

those British laws were tyrannical and unjust?" Emily continued.

Lavinia and Mr. MacKenzie both nodded. "When the laws of humankind create evil, we must keep our sights on the laws of God," Lavinia said gravely.

"That's certain," added Mr. MacKenzie. He pointed to Emily with his fork. "Our ancestor may have had a mixture of motives for wishing to defy those laws, but nevertheless, I can't fault him for doing it."

Emily looked from Lavinia to their father. The kitchen was warm and quiet, and scented with cherries and stewed lobster. She was sure the captured runaways would eat nothing but bitter sorrow that night.

"I believe the law which allowed those slaves to be caught today is wrong," she said in a low voice. "I can't believe that here in Massachusetts where independence began, those poor people can be captured and put in irons. It ain't right."

Lavinia reached across the table for Emily's hand. "I agree with you, dear."

"And so the laws which the Southerners live by, those slave states, those are wrong laws, too, ain't they?" Emily asked. She was glad for the comfort of her sister's hand. "And living in Massachusetts can't make us clear of their wrongness."

"Slavery is a sin," Mr. MacKenzie said. "And I need no minister to tell me that, no sermon to tell me that the laws upholding slavery are great wrongs. Slavery deforms and kills and defeats the hearts of those who are subject

118

to it, and works a terrible corrupting evil in the minds of those who profit by it."

"But Father—" Emily gulped hard. "Father, haven't we profited by it, too?"

He frowned. "In what way?"

Emily clenched her hands together in her lap, pressing down on one thumbnail until it turned dead white. Her voice quavered. "Our greatest prosperity came when MacKenzies were in shipping, and I expect they must have worked the slave trade, because nearly everyone did. And didn't this inn profit and prosper by selling rum? Ain't we as much to blame as, say, the Stockwells?"

There was silence in the kitchen. Coal shifted quietly in the stove, and in the distance, a firecracker went off, setting dogs barking.

Mr. MacKenzie crossed his knife and fork across his plate, wiped his mouth, and laid the napkin down with ceremonial slowness. A deep crease made a shadow between his eyebrows. He glanced at Lavinia as though asking her advice, and Lavinia nodded once.

Emily looked from one to the other in growing despair, wishing they would speak.

"Father?" she whispered.

"Emily," he said, scraping back his chair. "If in years past our family did gain even indirectly through slavery, that is only to our shame, and it is only that much more our duty to make recompense."

Emily thought of Moses, and there was no adventure in her imagining. "So we must act," she said.

Her father and sister were still silent, and a slow certainty awakened in her. Emily raised her eyes to her father's troubled, careworn face as a prickle of awareness crept up her spine.

"The hidey-hole," she wondered aloud. "Father, you have hidden runaways in this house, haven't you?"

He nodded. "Yes, Emily."

"Those times when I thought it locked or blocked or stuck, and you both were so angry with me . . ." She turned her gaze to Lavinia, and a dull flush spread up Emily's throat. She swallowed a bitter taste. "You must think me the biggest fool God ever made."

"No, dear, no," Lavinia said with a swift smile. "We never wanted you to know. We would not compel you to break the law along with us. We began this when you were a little child and never told you as you grew up."

Emily stared at the coal stove in the old stone hearth and shook her head from side to side. All the strange dreams of her childhood, of people slipping through the garden in the dark, of whispers and urgent instructions were dreams only because she had been too careless and unconsidering to recognize them for truth.

She sighed, and looked back at Lavinia. Her sister was watching her sadly, protectively.

"Oh, Lavvy," Emily cried, jumping up and running to the other side of the table. She threw her arms around her sister, and pressed her cheek to Lavinia's belly. Emily felt the baby kick against her face.

"I'm so bad and selfish." She gulped. "I've had such selfish thoughts."

"No, Emily. Don't be silly," Lavinia said, stroking

Emily's hair. "We didn't want you to know. We wanted to protect you."

"But I could have seen if I had opened my eyes." Emily choked. She caught her breath. "Does Lucy know?"

Lavinia's hand paused in its gentle stroking, and then resumed. "Yes, Lucy knows."

"Oh, I'm a fool, I'm a fool," Emily cried.

"Now, hush." Lavinia held Emily away from her and looked at her somberly. "Whether you ever noticed or not ain't important, not now. What is important is that you never change in your manner or conversation in the tavern. You must never, by any sign, indicate what Father and I have done here because we'll surely do it again."

"I guess you must have worried my big mouth would betray you if I knew," Emily said, another flush of mortification rushing up her throat. "Were those poor folks that got caught today—were they here?"

Lavinia nodded. "Yes. But we know we can trust you, Emily. You're grown-up, now. You know how careful we must be."

"I'll keep quiet," Emily promised. She sent her father an anxious look. "But the Stockwells—didn't you take a terrible risk putting them up?"

Mr. MacKenzie rubbed the stubble of beard on his chin and cheeks. "Well . . . it may seem so, but I prefer people to think we have only commercial motives and are glad to take anyone's money. Mr. Pinkham seemed less inquisitive about us once he saw the Stockwells were our guests."

With a wondering sigh, Emily returned to her chair.

Her father and Lavinia had a different appearance and aspect to her now, as though she had only seen flat daguerreotypes of them before, and saw them for the first time in the flesh.

"I'm all flittered," she admitted.

"Go on," Lavinia said kindly. "Go on and watch the fireworks, Em. I never wanted to burden you with this, and now that you know, I want you to put it out of your mind. Leave me and Father to worry about these things."

Reluctantly, Emily rose as she was told and walked to the door. There, she stopped to look back over her shoulder. Her father and sister were seated at the table, their hands illuminated by the glow of the whale-oil lamp and their faces in faint shadow.

"What will happen if you're found out?" she asked. "What if Mr. Pinkham keeps poking around?"

"It doesn't matter," Mr. MacKenzie said simply. "He doesn't frighten me. Now, go on, enjoy the fireworks."

Emily obeyed and left through the door to the garden. She stood at the gate, engulfed in the scent of roses, her mind drifting. In the darkened streets, boys ran, catcalling and twirling noisemakers, and girls giggled, their white dresses pale and ghostly in the twilight, the streaming ribbons in their hair fluttering like banners behind them. Breaking off a bloom, Emily slipped through the gate and followed the children. Their running footsteps echoed into silence, and Emily heard only her own soft tread.

A far-off explosion thudded like cannon fire, and a burst of brilliant light blazed over the harbor. Emily lifted her face to the sight. Reds, blues, and yellows flashed in a rain of stars, and the rattle of firecrackers punctuated the night like musket fire. The scent of burnt gunpowder drifted through the empty streets, carried by distant shouts and screams of excitement.

Emily stopped where an alley, framed by two warehouses, gave a narrow glimpse of the Harbor and the Neck on the other side. Torches shone in the darkness, and more and more explosions pounded the air, throbbing against Emily's breastbone like the thunder of battle.

She began to shiver. The future was suddenly a frightening blank and threatened loss.

"I must *do* something," she whispered, trying to stop shaking.

Up the alley from the harbor front walked a slim form silhouetted by the blazing sky. Emily did not need light to know who it was.

"Lucy." She cleared the roughness from her throat. "Lucy!"

Lucy paused, and then came on more slowly. Emily waited for her, wanting to reveal everything that was in her heart but not knowing how to do so. She felt a reserve between them that had never existed before. She twisted the stem of the rose between her fingers and waited nervously for her friend.

"Had enough of the show?" Emily asked as Lucy reached her.

"I hate a crowd."

Emily winced at the coolness in Lucy's voice. "We

should have taken the *Rosy* out and watched from the water," Emily said. "I wish I'd thought of it before."

"If you had, you wouldn't have asked me to go along," Lucy said.

"I don't know why you say that," Emily said. She swallowed a hard lump in her throat. "Lucy, you've changed toward me and I can't understand it."

Lucy was silent, watching the harbor. Emily could see her profile against a faint light from the warehouse window. Someone must be working with one lamp, hunched over ledgers, counting, keeping the appetite of hungry commerce satisfied.

"Lavinia and Father told me something tonight," Emily struggled on. Her fingers were sticky with sap. "I guess you know what it was all about. They said you've known for a long time what they're up to."

"Maybe I did."

"And you never told me?" Emily hated to hear the pitiful complaint in her own voice. She sounded puny and thin against the background of explosions and whistling rockets. "Didn't you think you could trust me?"

Lucy's silence brought tears to Emily's eyes.

"I admit you had reason not to," Emily faltered. "But you must believe me now when I say I want to help you get Moses away."

"I don't know what you're talking about." Lucy turned and began to walk off.

"What?" Emily stared openmouthed at her friend's retreating back, and felt her stomach roll over sickeningly. "You know what I mean, Lucy Sykes!"

At once, Lucy stopped and turned. "No, I do not know what you mean," she said. "You change your mind so many times, I don't think you know yourself what you're talking about, so I surely don't."

"Lucy!" Emily gulped air. She felt as though she'd fallen overboard, with the black water closing over her head. She reached out her hand, but Lucy backed away.

"I'll move out of our bedroom," Lucy said stiffly. "I think I'd rather sleep with Lavinia."

More gunsmoke drifted into the street, stinging Emily's eyes. She blinked tears away. "But we've always shared a bed."

"You might as well get used to the notion," Lucy replied. "You didn't think I'd be going with you to Virginia, did you?"

Emily was staggered. Lucy turned and hurried away, and was soon lost in the darkness. The fireworks continued to boom over the harbor, exploding like the shards of a friendship that had just been broken into pieces. One shell crashed right over Emily's head, and her hand clenched with a jerk, driving a thorn into her thumb. Emily burst into tears.

# Chapter Ten

EMILY PUSHED HERSELF through her chores the next morning, rubbing beeswax into the parlor furniture until the wood gleamed, and sweeping and scrubbing the tavern floor until her shoulderblades ached.

But no matter how hard she worked, she could not stop her mind from careening from one sore subject to the next. She felt ashamed of her own blind stupidity, and angry with Lucy for categorizing her with the Stockwells; and with that she had to struggle to overcome a vague resentment toward Lavinia for silently taking on so many burdens without offering to share.

"I'm not a baby, after all," she whispered, sitting back on her heels in a sea of suds. "There's plenty I could do to help."

Angry and hurt, Emily threw the scrub brush into her bucket hard enough to splash soapy water over the rim. Her thumb throbbed from where the rose had pricked her. She sucked on it morosely, and then gagged at the taste of soap.

"I'll probably get blood poisoning and die," she grumbled. "Then they'll be sorry."

What rankled almost as much as Lucy's rejection was that she'd been deliberately kept in the dark. Her father and Lavinia must have thought her too flighty or too reckless to be trusted, and they had shooed her out of the Wild Rose on many occasions—occasions for escape that had seemed like blessings at the time, but which Emily now realized were times when they simply wanted her out of the way.

"They want me out of the way, I'll just get out of the way," Emily muttered.

She opened the tavern door, stepped onto the street, and slammed the door shut with a resounding crash. She stood glaring at it, relishing the fit of morbid indignation she'd worked herself into. But her angers were never long-lasting, and it drained away even as she stood in the hot sun, glaring at her family's house. The inn loomed above her, mute and shut, and the closed door seemed like a closed mouth. It had nothing to say to her. Emily felt rejected from her own home.

With a sigh, she turned away and walked wearily down the street. Sparrows flitted across her path, and a man trundling a wheelbarrow full of clams passed her in the street. A cat perching on a windowsill sniffed the air as the clams went by, and then narrowed its gaze at Emily. She turned the corner to make for the Little Harbor, but for once the thought of taking out the *Rosy* didn't hearten her. If she went sailing, she would only be that much more isolated; what she wanted was someone to prize her and make her welcome. She made for the main harbor.

The port was as busy and noisy during the day as the Wild Rose was at night. Fast coastal schooners were berthed at the docks, and men came and went on the business of provisioning and unloading. Gulls yawked. A skinny, red-haired boy with a canvas bag slung over his shoulder stood in conference with a grizzled ship's mate, earnestly gesturing with his hands. A drunken woman walked with steady precision around a cartload of squealing pigs, and three men watched her, grinning and digging one another with their elbows. A skinny black man, stripped to the waist and shining with sweat, transferred sacks of flour from a wagon to a barrow.

Emily took it all in with the eyes of a stranger. Everyone but her had matters of importance, occupation, and purpose. She felt alone and outcast from her own place; the people she had thought she knew were not what they had seemed, and did not share their secrets with her but went forward without telling her where they were going, or when they would return. Her gaze roamed hungrily around the rigging of a clipper, wishing she could go with it to the far seas and be done with the battering confusions of her life.

To her left, a movement caught her attention. Emily saw Blount sitting on a coil of rope, rendering the harbor scene in his sketchbook. Her heart made a painful twisting inside her. For a moment, she watched him unobserved as she waged war inside her own heart and mind. He was a Southerner. His family owned slaves. With her own ears she had heard him profess his philosophy, and yet she could not credit it. Surely he could not be as kind, as good-natured, and as playful as he was if he truly believed those things.

Blount was different from the others. He must be, Emily pleaded to herself. Surely she could not feel the way she did about him if he honestly held those beliefs. Blount could not be committed to the institution which hunted down runaways and put them in irons. He could not do so and yet bring her a picnic and sympathize with her every emotion and transfer her image to paper as though every line of her face had been imprinted in his hand's memory from birth.

He had never been anything but sweet and generous and tender toward her. From the first, he had shown himself eager for her friendship and company, had sought her out and never asked for anything in return.

Slowly, Emily crossed the plank wharf toward him. As she drew closer, she could see his drawing, saw his fine-boned hand moving the pencil with short, careful strokes; then he suddenly drew a sweeping arabesque across the sketch.

"Oh, you've ruined it!" she cried out.

He turned, and stood up with a smile. "It was no good," he said. "Hello."

"Hello," she replied, cherishing the warmth in his voice. She clung to it like a life raft.

He made a gesture toward the coil of rope he had perched upon. "Won't you sit?"

"Thank you."

Emily lowered herself onto the rope, and the sharp hot smell of sun-warmed hemp prickled her nose. Looking up, she shielded her eyes against the sun's glare. It made a golden aura around Blount's head. "Why did you ruin your picture?" she asked. "I'm sure it was very good."

"Ah, no, it didn't suit me," Blount said, settling at her feet and examining his sketch with a critical eye.

Emily leaned over his shoulder to look at the picture. Then, as she watched, he turned the pages back. On every sheet were drawings of her. She knew he had drawn her aboard her boat, but there were sketches of her in the tavern, in the garden, on the street, in moods and poses when she had been utterly unaware of his attention. The delicacy and grace of the portraits brought a blush to her cheek. The pictures proclaimed more clearly than words could do: he loved her.

"I hope you don't mind," Blount said quietly.

Emily shook her head. For a moment, she could not speak, so powerful was the impression that he had looked into her heart. "No," she whispered when she had mastered herself somewhat. "I think you have done me a real compliment."

"I only draw what I see."

He turned around to look up at her, and Emily suddenly wished they were both far away, away from the crowd and noise of the harbor.

"No one ever treated me so nice before," Emily said

with a catch in her voice. She twisted her hands together in her lap. "I just—I like you so, and I wish you weren't going away at the end of the summer."

"I wish it, too," Blount said hoarsely. "But perhaps we won't part, after all."

Emily understood him perfectly and her heart ached with wanting and uncertainty.

Three mariners began a heated argument nearby, and their raucous voices broke the fragile thing that shimmered in the air between Emily and Blount. Emily drew in a shaky breath and stood. Blount rose, too, frowning at the interruption.

"How are you finding the Ship?" Emily asked. They began walking away from the noisy harbor.

"Oh, comfortable enough," he said. "My parents seem to like it, but it seems a lonely place to me."

"Because I'm not there?"

"Because you're not there," he agreed.

Their way brought them to the back of Handys' inn. The yard was enclosed with a high stockade fence, hiding the garden from the street. Music from a badly tuned piano came from a hidden window, but a woman's voice sang "Sweet Betsy from Pike" sweetly and truly. Emily stood aside as Blount reached to open the gate.

"I won't go in," she said. "My family and the Handys have a history of not liking one another, so I'll say good-bye to you here."

Blount nodded. "I understand. If you can get away tomorrow, let's go sailing."

"I'd like that," Emily said. "I'll try."

He looked at her for a moment, and then bent to kiss her cheek. Emily touched his arm and closed her eyes and heard the sweet singing on the warm air.

"Until tomorrow," he whispered.

Blount pushed open the gate, but then halted. Framed by the open gateway, standing by a bed of young cabbages, were Lucy and Moses, holding hands. They stood frozen, staring at Emily and Blount.

Then, before any of them spoke, the back door opened and Mr. Stockwell stepped out. He took one look at Moses and Lucy and turned wrathfully dark.

"Get out of here, girl," he growled.

Lucy did not move.

"Moses, you stupid black bastard, get that horse of mine and be quick about it," Mr. Stockwell said with deadly calm. "And don't bring your sluts here."

The blood raced to Emily's face.

"How dare you?" she demanded. "She's my sister!"

Mr. Stockwell ignored her. "Be quick, Moses, or you'll be sorry."

Moses released Lucy's hand. He had to pass Mr. Stockwell to reach the stable, and as he did so, the man kicked him hard and sent him sprawling.

Lucy stood motionless, staring at Mr. Stockwell, and Emily feared something terrible might happen. She darted in and grabbed Lucy's hand, hauling her out through the gate. As she left, she saw Blount send her an apologetic glance.

"Let go of me," Lucy said, wrenching her arm away from Emily as they hurried down the street.

"No, I will not," Emily said through gritted teeth. She pushed open the gate to another garden and yanked Lucy inside, off the street. Then she let go, and Lucy stood trembling, her eyes wide with anger and outrage. She stared at Emily in disgust.

"I don't know why you seem to blame me," Emily said, feeling her own anger rise.

"No, I guess you don't."

"Lucy." Emily's voice broke. "I don't know what's happened, but I hate it. I don't know why we aren't friends anymore."

When Lucy didn't reply, Emily felt a sweeping tiredness wash over her. Shaking her head, she turned and walked out through the gate again and up the street. But with each slow step, two painful questions repeated themselves in her head: Why didn't Blount stop his father? Why didn't *she*?

She stopped and looked back over her shoulder. Emily knew her friend would never trust her again, and that loss hurt as much as anything else ever had. All her procrastination and equivocation had been prompted by a wish to save Lucy, but the result was quite the opposite. She had lost her friend as surely as if Lucy had slipped off the edge of the world.

If there was any shred of hope at all, however, Emily knew it lay in her making a decision and staying with it. Instead of changing course to suit the wind, she must pick one point and steer by it, no matter what.

"Tell the wind where you want to go and make it take you there," Emily said under her breath.

She closed her eyes for a moment. Sailing in the dark meant fixing a star, but they were very far away, and she was painfully aware that she would have no companion.

It was too hurtful to speculate how her feelings for Blount had colored her judgment and sapped her will, but she knew that they had. Deafening herself to the clamorous confusion in her heart, Emily hitched up her skirts and ran to find her minister. She raced up the alley and burst out onto Elm Street. Two hounds began baying hysterically as she sprinted past their house. Then, as she dodged around another corner, a horse reared, kicking out with its front hooves.

"Whoa! Watch out, girl!" the startled rider yelled.

Emily ducked under the flailing hooves and ran straight for the Polks' front door. She pounded upon it wildly, frantic to take action. She was both furious and brokenhearted, and did not dare stop for fear of losing courage. "Mr. Polk!" she cried. "Mr. Polk!"

The door opened suddenly, and Emily almost fell in across the doorstep. Mrs. Polk, cowled in a black lace bonnet, stood blinking at her. "Emily MacKenzie! What is the meaning of this racket? You nigh scared the wits out of me!"

Emily gulped for breath. "Please, I must talk to Mr. Polk. It's awful urgent."

"He's working on his sermon for next Sunday," the woman replied doubtfully. Her head shook as she spoke, and the wattles under her chin quivered with uncertainty. "I hardly like to interrupt him."

"Please." Emily fought hard for composure. "I have a matter of great spiritual—um—I need to talk—"

She broke off, hearing footsteps in the hall. Desperately she looked beyond Mrs. Polk's shoulder and saw the minister standing in the door of his study.

"Come in, Emily," Mr. Polk said.

Emily almost sobbed with relief. She slipped past an astonished Mrs. Polk and followed her minister into his sanctum. He seated himself behind his desk, gesturing toward a chair. Emily pulled it forward and sat on the edge. Her knuckles were cut and smarted like beestings, but she ignored the pain.

"Sir," she panted. "Do you remember what we spoke of at the Wild Rose last week?"

He nodded. The light coming through his window made a glare on his spectacles, hiding his eyes.

"I'm in dire need to know, sir," Emily said. "I know what role my family has played in getting slaves away, so I'm not as ignorant as I was, but please, I have to know. What would have happened to those runaways if they hadn't gotten caught?"

He was silent, and Emily felt a chill as she stared at the blank lenses of his spectacles. They made him as inscrutable as a statue. Then he leaned forward out of the light and was his benignant self again. He regarded her for a long moment, judging and weighing carefully.

"They were to wait for a ship that comes in tomorrow," Mr. Polk said at last. "The captain is Thayer Trelawney, and he was to take them to Nova Scotia."

Emily squeezed her hands between her knees to

keep them from shaking. "Then he must have berth and provision now that the others are not going. Sir, I have cargo for that space."

"Do you indeed?" Mr. Polk pursed his mouth for a moment. "Don't you think you should entrust this cargo to your father, Emily?"

Her heart made a painful lurch. "No, sir, I've got to take care of this myself."

"Mmhmm." The minister frowned down at the papers spread across the green baize desktop, as though seeking guidance from his scriptural notes. The clock ticked in time with Emily's heart.

"How long will he be in port?" Emily pressed.

"That I can't tell you, for I don't know," Mr. Polk replied quietly. He looked up at Emily and gave her a searching look.

"Do you know what will happen to your cargo if, once you begin, you falter in the slightest? This is a venture which must be carried to completion once begun. You may not change your course."

Emily nodded. She licked her lips. "I know."

The minister rose and motioned for her to precede him to the door. Emily obeyed, not knowing if he supported her or not.

"I will speak to Captain Trelawney when he makes port," Mr. Polk said, one hand on the doorknob. "But only he can say yea or nay."

"I understand." Emily bowed her head as Mr. Polk opened the door for her.

The solemn atmosphere of the minister's house was

like a heavy cape around her shoulders, but as soon as Emily stepped out onto the street and into the sunshine, she felt her spirits lift. Surely Lucy would forgive her now, now that Emily had the means to convey Moses to freedom. Then things would be as they once were between them.

With growing excitement, Emily hurried back to the Wild Rose. She could hear the low murmur of voices from the tavern, as steady as the breaking of waves on the beach. She snatched her apron off a peg, and tying it around her, went in search of Lucy.

"Emily, there you are." Lavinia turned the corner of the hallway. She was holding two filled lamps in her hands. "Take these in, will you?"

"Is Lucy here?" Emily asked impatiently, taking the lamps.

"In the tavern, helping Father."

Emily backed through the door to the main room, and the babble of voices rose around her. The first afternoon patrons were already taking relief from the day's heat, and several men called greetings to Emily as she made her way between the tables.

Lucy stood behind the bar beside Mr. MacKenzie, placing full mugs of beer on a tray. She glanced up at Emily but said nothing.

"Lucy," Emily whispered as she set the lamps down on the bar. She leaned close. "I have to talk to you."

"I'm busy," Lucy said, ducking under the partition and then lifting the heavy tray.

137

"It can wait, I *must* speak to you now," Emily said under her breath.

Lucy raised her chin. "Is that an order?"

"Oh! Merciful God!" Emily shouted.

The conversations stopped abruptly. The men turned startled eyes on Emily. Her face burned. After sending the room at large a weak smile, she turned back to Lucy.

"Will you please step outside with me. Please? Or would you like me to go on screaming?" She widened her eyes and jerked her head toward the door.

Grudgingly, Lucy set down the tray, and the two girls stepped outside the inn. Horse-and-buggy teams whisked by, the whirring wheels making a clickety-click over the broken clamshells in the street. Pedestrians ambled by on their business, mothers leading children by the hand, men walking with their heads together over negotiations. There was a general air of business and purpose, as though everyone in town had a plan and was intent on carrying it through. The noise of the street was enough to obscure the girls' voices, but Emily spoke low, just to be safe.

"Now, Lucy," she began excitedly. "I know you think I've been an awful fool, and I guess I have, but now I got it all cleared up. There's a ship coming in tomorrow that can take Moses up to Nova Scotia. I don't have it all worked out yet, but you tell Moses that he's got to be ready anytime because I don't know how long Captain Trelawney will stay here."

She stopped breathlessly, waiting with an eager smile

138

for the good news to sink in. Lucy's face was expression-less.

"Don't you understand what I'm telling you?" Emily said. "He can get free!"

Lucy sucked one of her eyeteeth and gazed up at the rooflines. "I don't know what you're talking about, but I have work to do."

Emily gaped in astonishment as Lucy turned to go back inside.

"No!" Emily jumped in front of Lucy to bar the door. "Don't you do this! Don't you be so angry at me that you ruin his chances."

Lucy narrowed her eyes. "How dare you say I'd ruin his chances?"

"Easy!" Emily retorted. "I just did. Now, you've just got to trust me, Lucy. You've got to tell him."

"I don't trust you and I won't tell him," Lucy growled.

"Then I'll go find him and tell him myself," Emily said.

Lucy laughed incredulously. "You think he'd believe a thing you told him?"

"Maybe he would," Emily said.

"Never." Lucy made to open the door.

"Then you tell him," Emily begged, all bluster and defiance gone. "There's no knowing if there will be an-other chance. It may be tomorrow, or maybe the day af-ter. But he's got to be ready and you've got to tell him."

Lucy stood poised on the doorstep, her head low-ered. Emily could see the pulse beat hard at her temple.

"Trust me," Emily whispered.

Lucy looked at her, her brown eyes unreadable and shuttered. Defeated, Emily stepped back.

"I am clean out of arguments, Lucy," Emily said. "There ain't another thing more I can say."

"I'll think about it," Lucy said at last. Then she went inside. The door clicked shut.

Emily let out a gasp of relief and leaned against the side of the inn. The wood was as warm at her back as a living thing. She let the warmth spread across her shoulders like an embrace, closing her eyes and letting the tension flow from her.

"Well, well, having a nap outdoors, Emily?"

Emily's eyes flew open. Micah sat astride the Ship's bay pacer, grinning down at her. Emily gave him a sour smile.

"Yes, I saw you coming and I was bored to exhaustion," she said.

Micah's grin widened, and the bay horse pawed the ground. Emily folded her arms. "Are you planning on stirring up a cloud of dust here or what? I wasn't looking to wash the windows tomorrow. Don't you have any business at home?"

"Less and less business all the time, I'm afraid," he said with false melancholy. "Our visitors from Richmond have decided that Marblehead is too salty for their taste, and they leave for Saratoga in two days."

Emily felt a jolt that left her fingertips tingling with alarm. "The Stockwells? They're leaving?" she wailed.

"Day after tomorrow," Micah said dryly. "You sure look disappointed."

"Well—I—" Emily's mind raced. She had only twenty-four hours to get Moses safely away.

"Yes," Micah continued. His heels swung back against the horse's flanks, but he kept the bay in check with the reins. It danced impatiently as Micah looked down at Emily. "You sure will miss that son of the South, won't you? I guess you'll have to steer *yourself* around mud puddles from now on."

Emily felt a hard knot of anger twist inside her. "You think you know just about everything, don't you? Go on, get out of here," she said. "You Handys are all alike."

"I'm pierced to the heart," Micah said. He made a mocking bow from the saddle. "Good day, Miss MacKenzie. Don't worry, I'm sure they'll be back next summer."

His hands moved forward on the horse's neck, and the bay sprang forward. Emily stood as still as a statue as the dust settled around her. She refused to think about what Micah had said. If she let her feelings for Blount obscure her vision yet again, she knew she'd be lost. Drawing a deep breath, Emily squared her shoulders and returned to the Wild Rose.

# Chapter Eleven

As soon as Emily awoke the next morning, her heart began a wild, panicked beating. She gripped the covers to her chin and squeezed her eyes shut tight as she willed herself to calm down. When her pulse settled, Emily rose slowly from the bed and padded to the tiny window.

She could see the tips of masts swaying gently to and fro in the harbor, and the silent, steady, outward flight of gulls to the ocean. She felt as though she herself were about to embark on a voyage as frightening as any whaling ship had ever made.

Emily closed her eyes and tried to pray. Her hands gripped the windowsill so hard her knuckles turned white, and she slowly sank to her knees.

"Help me," she whispered. "What am I doing?"

From below her on the street, she heard a gentle humming. Emily looked down to see a woman crooning gently to a baby held in her arms. "That's my brave girl," the mother said quietly. "Don't cry."

Emily felt calmness and resolution settle upon her. She followed the mother and child with her eyes until they turned the corner, her mind filled with long-ago images and her ear hearing a far-off lullaby. Then she dressed and went downstairs to begin the day.

"Any ships come in this tide?" she asked, stepping into the kitchen and tying on her apron.

"Not as I know," Lavinia replied.

Emily swung open the oven door and poked at the ashes with a piece of kindling from the box. She saw that her hands were shaking again. She gripped the wood tighter.

"Good morning!"

"Oh!" Emily's hand jerked against the warm stove. She looked around guiltily to see her father.

"Jumpy as a cat this morning, Em," Mr. MacKenzie said jovially. He rubbed his hands together. "Let's start some coffee brewing, girls."

"Yes, Father," Emily replied shakily.

Lavinia gave her a puzzled look. "Are you feeling poorly?"

"No, not at all," Emily said with a quick shake of her head. "I'm as right as rain. I'll go get us some eggs."

She hurried outside and went into the dim, straw-scented shed. The hens clucked and complained as she felt among the roosting boxes, and Emily hoped from one minute to the next that Captain Trelawney would make port, and then fleetingly hoped that he wouldn't. If only the responsibility were taken from her.

She stopped groping in the straw as her hand turned over two brown eggs. In a moment, Emily pictured Moses delicately touching the eggs in his basket. She remembered the shadow of his lashes on his dark cheek and the gentle gravity of his voice. He did not deserve his fate. No one did. She shuddered.

Emily emerged from the outbuilding holding one egg in either hand, and she cast a wary glance at the back of the rambling Wild Rose Inn. The windows were blank with the morning glare. She wondered if Lucy was upstairs sweeping the hallway, and if she might be looking out and seeing Emily standing there. She wondered what Lucy might think.

She knew, however, that it did not matter what Lucy thought of her; it did not matter if she had lost Lucy's trust and love. It was a bitter loss, but what mattered was to help Moses escape.

Emily bowed her head. If Trelawney did not come, she must find another way.

Someone let out a low, hailing whistle. Startled, she looked toward the gate. Blount stood on the other side, almost completely obscured by the full-flushed roses. Emily felt as though someone had her heart and was squeezing the life out of it. She couldn't speak.

"Good morning," Blount said, opening the gate and stepping through with an easy smile. "I wonder if we might get in a sail today?"

"Oh, I don't—I can't say," Emily faltered. She bent

her head over the pair of eggs. Her heart beat wildly as he walked toward her. She wanted to run, but couldn't.

"Emily?"

Emily thought for a moment that she might cry. She knew she was preparing to repay his kindness and affection with betrayal, and that she would lose not only his company the next day, but his regard and his love as well. If she could have found a way to explain, to assure him of how much she cared for him, she would have done so. But she couldn't, and he would leave, believing that she had never loved him at all.

"Emily, I hoped we could go sailing today," he said in a roughened voice. "I'm sorry, we leave tomorrow."

"I know," she whispered, still looking down. "But—"

"Don't say 'but,'" Blount broke in urgently. "Please. We won't have another chance."

For a moment, Emily's throat was so tight with tears that she thought she would choke. She shook her head. "I can't," she whispered.

"Why?"

She didn't answer. She felt the worst traitor in the world.

"Emily, why?"

At last, she raised her head to look at him. There was no mischief or laughter in his eyes anymore, only regret and sadness. He stepped forward, his hand raised as though to caress her cheek.

"No," Emily gasped, turning aside blindly.

Blount's hand dropped to his side. "I beg your pardon," he said with stiff formality.

Emily looked at him pleadingly. "Oh, Blount, I didn't mean—"

"Emily?" Lavinia opened the back door.

"I have to go." With one last apologetic look at Blount, Emily hurried to the house.

"You've another visitor," Lavinia said, glancing across the garden at Blount. She looked at Emily. "It's Captain Trelawney."

Emily's heart skipped a beat and then began to pound heavily. "Where is he?" she asked hoarsely.

"In the tavern."

With flushed cheeks, Emily brushed past her sister and hurried to the taproom, still holding the eggs.

Seated by the cold fireplace was a swarthy, gray-haired seaman in seaboots and a weather-stained coat. A cup of coffee steamed on the table before him. Emily stared at him speechlessly. She felt crippled and encumbered by her fragile burden, afraid to run and unable to use her hands.

"I'm looking for Emily MacKenzie," Captain Trelawney said. He had the low, cautious voice of a man who dealt with secrets.

"I'm her," Emily replied. She nudged the door shut with her foot.

"I paid a call on my minister this morning," Captain Trelawney said, giving her a quick scrutiny. He sipped his coffee and smacked his lips with satisfaction. "This coffee is fine."

Emily tried to steady her breathing. "Sir—"

He set the cup down with a thump. "Mr. Polk tells me you have cargo for my ship?"

"Yes, yes, I do," Emily agreed. "Where should we—"

The captain turned his head away quickly, as though telling her not to say too much. "You must deliver your cargo this evening," he said in his low, measured tone. "The tide turns at eight o'clock. You know what that means."

"Yes," Emily said, nodding once. "You will not wait."

"I will not wait." Captain Trelawney took another sip of coffee, and then stood up. "Ship's name is *Freedom*." He opened the street door, stepped out, and was gone.

Emily waited for a moment to quiet her racing heart. The door behind her to the passage opened. Emily looked around.

Lucy stood framed in the doorway. "That was him?"

Emily nodded. "Yes. Lucy, do you believe I am in earnest? I never did harm on purpose, you know that. You *know* that."

"I know it," Lucy replied softly. She looked down at her hands, twining her fingers together. When Lucy looked up again, Emily saw there were tears in her eyes. "But I'm scared to death."

"Oh, Lucy." Emily sighed. "I guess you love Moses."

Lucy nodded. "I do."

"We'll get him away," Emily whispered. "You'll see."

Lucy straightened up and brushed a tear from her cheek. "Yes, I'll see," she said in a low voice.

Emily felt a quiver of uneasiness. "You do trust me, don't you?" she asked.

"Sure, Emily." Lucy turned and went back into the hallway, leaving Emily in the empty tavern. The captain's coffee mug sat on the table, the steam rising into the air like unspoken doubts. Emily carefully walked back outside and returned the eggs to their nest.

The tavern began to fill with patrons at five-thirty. Emily watched the clock, astonished at how unevenly the time seemed to go. When Lavinia rang the dinner bell at six, Emily let out an inadvertent cry of alarm.

"Don't worry, Emily. I'll save you some pie!" Mr. Ledue cackled as he hightailed it for the dining room.

Emily met Lucy in the kitchen and they exchanged glances as they both hoisted heavy trays. Emily raised her eyebrows to look a question, and Lucy nodded just slightly.

"He's ready," Lucy said.

With her heart knocking behind her ribs, Emily carried dinner into the dining room and set the dishes down on the long table, with a curious sense of unreality. She heard her own voice respond to the friendly bickering of the daily patrons, saw her own hands and Lucy's hands arranging plates of waffles and jugs of syrup, but she felt as though she were watching things from a remove. When she had placed the last platter of fried pork chops on the board, Emily slipped out of the dining room.

She ducked her head through the kitchen door. "I have to step out for a moment," she said and popped out before Lavinia could answer. Laughter came from the taproom, where her father stayed to serve those people who weren't eating dinner. Outside, Emily swiftly headed for the Ship.

*Emily MacKenzie is going to steal a slave,* she told herself in astonishment. Her footsteps sounded unusually loud in the empty dinner-hour streets, and the housefronts looming up on either side seemed like so many watching faces. Emily quickened her pace and turned the corner.

Before her was the Ship. The Handys' house was as old as her own home and as much of a hodgepodge as the Wild Rose Inn, but it bore new paint and wore an unmistakable air of prosperity. For two centuries, the two establishments had been rivals, and the families at odds. The fortunes of each had waxed and waned, but lately the Ship had been steadily fattening and the Wild Rose growing lean. Emily fought down the bitterness that rose in her whenever she thought of the Handys, and opened the door.

Inside the common room, well-dressed men sat with glasses of wine under an abundance of gleaming lamplight. One man was showing off a scale model of a racing yacht, his face flushed with the pride of ownership. Smoke from expensive cigars filled the air. Micah was seated opposite a fat man in a silk waistcoat, his smile blandly attentive. As Emily stood there on the threshold, he looked up and met her eyes. If he was surprised to see her, he gave no sign of it.

"Why, Emily," Micah said with a smile. He rose to meet her. "Welcome to our humble—"

"Where's Blount Stockwell?" Emily broke in clumsily.

Micah's face went blank. "In the garden with a book of verse," he replied. "I'll fetch him for you."

"No, don't," Emily said firmly. She started forward, and then stopped in confusion. "I'm sorry—where?"

"Straight back through the passageway," Micah said curtly as he turned back into the room.

A sudden wave of confusion and shame made Emily pause. She looked at Micah's back as he left, but couldn't think of what she could say to him, or if there was anything to say at all. Emily knew she owed him nothing and need not explain herself, yet she almost wanted to. But then a glimpse of a tall-case clock in the corner recalled her purpose to her and she hurried away.

The windowless hallway stretched straight back through the house to a heavy door. Emily fumbled in the dimness for the latch, found it, and pushed the door open to the garden. Beneath the same tree where Lucy and Moses had courted, Blount sat on the grass, reading. When he saw Emily, he sprang to his feet and cast the book aside.

"Emily!" His face was lit with pleasure.

Emily quailed before his obvious happiness and her own deceit. "I've come to ask a favor," she said haltingly.

"Anything."

His ready generosity made Emily feel even worse. "I'd like to borrow Moses," she told him. "That captain who came this morning said he would deliver something for me, but I have to get it to his ship—and so—"

"And so you'd like Moses to take it for you," Blount finished for her. He frowned solemnly. "You may borrow him, but you must pay for the use of him."

Emily's face flooded with color. "What?"

"Take me on an evening sail," Blount said. He caught her hand eagerly. "You told me once what an adventure it is, and this is our last chance."

Emily's mind raced. The last place she wanted Blount to be that evening was in the harbor where Trelawney's ship was. But she saw little choice. Swallowing hard, she looked at Blount and nodded. "Very well. Let me see my cargo safely stowed, and I'll meet you at the *Rosy* in half an hour."

"Wonderful." Blount looked as happy as a puppy. "I'll find Moses and send him to your house. He's around here somewhere. But why don't I come with you now?"

"No!" Emily's pulse tripped wildly as she searched her imagination for an excuse. Instantly, she lit on the one excuse that would appease him.

"I—I want to change my dress and—and—" Emily felt sick with shame as she saw the flattered delight in his eyes.

Blount smiled. "I'll see you in half an hour, then," he said, pressing her hand. "Let me find Moses for you."

Emily wanted to scream or tear her dress or kick something as she watched Blount go in search of his family's slave. She had never felt so despicable nor so regretful.

"I'm sorry," she whispered, turning and fleeing back into the house. Emily ran blindly through the passageway as though all the furies of Hell were chasing her. She stumbled to a halt at the entrance, yanked open the front door and almost fell out onto the street. Panting, Emily shut the door and put her back to it. Her knees were shaking. Above her, the sky was deepening, and the evening breeze whispered across her hot forehead.

"Miss Emily?"

Blinking back tears, Emily turned. Moses had rounded the corner of the house, and now walked to her. He knew he was about to sail for Canada, yet had nothing but the clothes he stood up in. He could take nothing with him without arousing suspicion. There was no other way to proceed. And so he stood there with empty hands, about to step into the unknown.

"Moses," Emily whispered.

"You want me to tote something for you?" he asked in a calm voice.

She nodded mechanically, aware of the need to keep up the charade. "Yes, come with me," she said, pushing herself away from the door and walking unsteadily up the street.

Moses walked beside her, no trace of fear in his face. Emily glanced at him from the corner of her eye, amazed by his composure. She was nearly stumbling with apprehension.

"Don't be scared," Moses said, looking straight ahead as they went. "I ain't."

"Why not?" Emily whispered.

He sent her a quick smile. "I've been scared almost

152

all my life, but not tonight. I ain't got nothing to lose. Only my freedom to gain."

While Moses continued walking, Emily stopped in the street and stared after him. Then, with a faint, hopeful smile, she followed and caught up to him, and they were silent the rest of the way.

When they reached Front Street, the Wild Rose Inn came into view. Lucy was watching out for them at the garden gate, her eyes huge. Beside her was a large crate on a barrow. The petals of one spent rose had fallen onto the crate and lay scattered on its surface like drops of blood.

"Moses, here's that load I want you to carry for me," Emily said in a loud, clear voice. "I want it taken to the harbor to Captain Trelawney. I'll show you. Come on, Lucy, you come too."

With a reassuring nod for Lucy, Moses lifted the handles of the wheelbarrow and set off down the street. Lucy hurried to keep up.

Watching them go, Emily found that her palms were slick with sweat. She hoped they had said their good-byes already, for they would not be able to do so at the harbor. Emily rubbed her hands on her apron and glanced back at the house. It had never looked so inviting before, in spite of its worn gray shabbiness. Laughter drifted from the windows with the smell of burning whale oil. Emily felt the breath catch in her throat.

Then she turned her back on the house and ran down the street after Lucy and Moses. A rock skittered away from her running feet and clicked sharply against a stone doorstep across the way. Lucy sent Emily a wary glance.

"Now, Moses," Emily said in an undertone. "When we reach the *Freedom,* don't stop. Just keep on right up the gangway with the barrow and leave me talk to whatever crew's there. I know Captain Trelawney has done this before and so there's some routine or other. Let's just do whatever he says."

"Yes, miss," Moses said quietly.

Lucy was silent. The barrow's wheel wobbled drunkenly and grated on its axle with harsh, intermittent squeaks that set Emily's teeth on edge. She could not stop herself from looking back over her shoulder every few feet.

"Quit that," Lucy whispered.

Emily nodded guiltily. "I can't help it." She gulped down a wave of panic.

As the street curved around to the harbor, the masts and halyards of Trelawney's ship came into sight, each line edged with gold from the westering sun, so that it looked as though it had been made with fire.

"I'm just as nervous as can be," Emily chattered on. "I just wish I—"

She froze, staring at the docks and the men busying around the *Freedom.* At the foot of the gangway, the bounty hunter stood smoking a pipe and jawing with two sailors. Lucy saw him at the same time and reached instantly for Moses's arm. On deck, Captain Trelawney stood facing the town. The offshore breeze lifted the gray

154

hair from his brow, revealing an angry scowl. Below, Pinkham guffawed over his conversation.

"What's wrong?" Moses asked in a low voice. He set the barrow down and looked at both girls.

"That man," Emily said. She clenched her fists so hard her nails dug into her palms. "It's that bounty hunter, and he's sure to ask you what you're doing if you go aboard."

"There's a plenty of Negro sailors," Moses said reasonably as he eyed the ship. "He won't know I ain't got a right to be there."

Lucy shook her head. "No," she whispered. "Don't risk it."

"Why, Lucy," Moses said in surprise, "you know I won't get another chance."

"No." Lucy shook her head. "They'll mutilate you or kill you or send you to Alabama." Her voice broke. "I'd die."

"Lucy, I'll die if I have to stay a slave," Moses said, tenderly cupping her cheek with one hand.

Lucy closed her eyes and pressed her face against his palm, and two tears slipped from between her lids. Emily's heart ached for them.

"Wait here," she said. "I'll talk to Trelawney, see what he says."

Drawing a deep breath, Emily headed for the ship. Sailors passed back and forth as she threaded her way among the bales of stores and cargo that sat on the wharf. She did not dare look at the bounty hunter directly, but she could see him from the corner of her vision. She saw him laugh and scratch himself and thump one of his companions on the back. All the time, she had a disturbing certainty that he was keeping an eye on Moses and Lucy. Emily kept her own eyes on the ship, superstitiously convinced that if she did not look at Pinkham, he would not notice her or take note of her actions. Her pulse raced.

"Hey, missy," he said just as she passed. "I see you got yourself two niggers up there."

She faced him slowly. "What if I do?"

He hawked and spat over the edge of the wharf into the water. "Well . . . Somebody of a suspicious frame of mind might wonder whatcher planning, seeing as how this ship is about to cut loose."

"I assume only one such as you could have such a low, suspicious mind," Emily said stiffly.

Pinkham grinned, showing tobacco-stained teeth. "I'd say, considering as how you're one of those Wild Rose MacKenzies, I believe I'm right to have a doubt about you."

Fear prickled Emily's fingertips. "I beg your pardon?"

"And that nigger gal of yours, she's from the same place, too." Pinkham walked around Emily in a circle, still grinning. "I got my nagging doubts about that whole parcel of you MacKenzies."

Fear and elation struggled within Emily's heart. She was terrified, but proud to be counted with her family as a slave smuggler. She gave Pinkham a cool stare.

"If it were in my power to thwart you, I would not

hesitate to do so," she said, throwing her head back. "And if you accost my sister again, I'll kill you."

"Hoo-hoo!" Pinkham laughed and looked back at the two young sailors with a grin. "She's a feisty young lady."

Captain Trelawney stood at the top of the gangway. "Let the lady by, mister," he warned.

Rigid with tension, Emily climbed up the gangway. Her muscles jumped and quivered with nervousness. Beneath her feet, the gangway was worn smooth with traffic, and the wooden cleats across it felt loose and slippery. Emily almost feared she would pitch into the water, but Trelawney reached down to her and hauled her unceremoniously onto deck. Deep lines of frustration cut into his forehead and down his cheeks from his nose to the corners of his mouth.

"Do you see him up there?" Emily muttered. "With the wheelbarrow. I thought he could bring it on board and—"

"Shh." Trelawney strode to the stern and leaned over the taffrail to yell an order at one of his sailors. He gestured for Emily to join him there, out of earshot of the bounty hunter.

"It is too risky to bring him aboard with that skunk lurking around," Captain Trelawney said. "Already he has questioned all my hands what course we take and what cargo we carry. It's not to be done."

"But Captain," Emily begged, putting a hand on his arm. "Is there some other way?"

The seaman squinted at the sky and then at the dark and shifting water. Emily had time to notice the peppering of gray in his beard stubble, and to watch the cook's boy come up a companionway and throw a bucket of slops over the side. Across the harbor, Marblehead Neck rode like a humped whale in a golden sea, the setting sun blazing off of distant windows. She refused to believe that her plan could fail, after all.

"I'll lie to, off the Neck for one hour," Trelawney muttered after a pause. "Get a boat and get him out there, and I'll take him. That is all I can do."

Emily looked at him searchingly. He was fierce and full of strange anger, as though he did not like what he was doing yet was compelled nevertheless to do so. She did not wait to delve into his motives, however. Hurrying back down the bouncing gangway, she ran past Pinkham and rejoined Moses and Lucy. She did not look at Lucy, but straight at Moses.

"Take the crate on board," she told him urgently. "Then you must come back and the ship will sail."

Moses raised his eyes to the sky. "Then I stay a slave," he whispered.

"No, wait." Emily shook her head. "The ship will wait for you on the far side of that land across the harbor. But for now, you must continue to deliver this, so that that man can see we have no secret purpose."

"Emily, I don't like this," Lucy began. "We'll find another—"

"I understand," Moses interrupted, picking up the handles of the wheelbarrow again.

He trundled the crate down onto the wharf. Emily and Lucy stood in the shadows, watching as he passed by the bounty hunter. Pinkham stared hard at Moses and then followed him up onto the ship.

"God, Jesus God," Lucy whispered.

Trelawney gestured toward the quarterdeck and said something in reply to the bounty hunter. Emily could almost hear the violence of Lucy's hatred and frustration, and she felt for her friend's hand. In helpless silence, they watched hand in hand as Moses trundled the empty wheelbarrow down off the ship again, and made his way back to them.

The bounty hunter walked slowly down the gangplank, and then stood on the wharf as the sailors cast off the lines. There was a creaking and straining as the topsails were unfurled, and the shouted commands of captain and mate came thinly against the breeze. Moses rejoined the girls in the deepening shadow, and the *Freedom* slowly moved away from the wharf.

# Chapter Twelve

 LUCY WAS THE first to drag her eyes from the retreating ship. When she turned on Emily, her expression was bleak and forbidding.

"You said to trust you," she said in a warning voice. "We trusted you."

"And you must keep on trusting me," Emily pleaded. She glanced furtively at the harbor, where the bounty hunter was standing alone, filling his pipe and following the ship's progress with narrowed eyes.

"What should I do?" Moses asked.

Emily took Lucy's arm. "Lead him out to the end of the Neck," she said quietly. "But hurry. You know how long it takes to get all the way out there."

"And you?" Lucy asked uncertainly.

"I'll bring the *Rosy* across the harbor and tie up on one of the rocks," Emily said. "When I do, you two must be ready to board her and sail out to meet Trelawney."

"But you'll lose your boat," Lucy whispered.

160

"No, for you'll be bringing it back."

Lucy shook her head. "I'm going with Moses," she said, clenching her jaw hard.

The color ebbed from Emily's face. "Lucy . . . Lucy, no!" She felt tears spring to her eyes and could not stop them from spilling out onto her cheeks. "But this is your home!" she quavered. "How can you leave?"

"Emily." Lucy's voice was tender toward her for the first time in weeks. She took both of Emily's hands in hers and waited for Emily to look at her. "This is *your* home. I can't abide a country that has slavery in it any longer. I'm going to start over in Canada. With Moses."

"Don't leave *me*!" Emily clutched Lucy's hands in mounting panic.

Gently, Lucy pulled away from Emily's grip. "Give my love to Uncle Marcus and Lavvy," she whispered, blinking away a tear. "I do wish I could see the baby, but I know he'll be beautiful. Good-bye, Em."

As Emily stood in tearful dismay, Lucy swiftly kissed her cheek, and then turned to Moses. "We have to hurry."

Side by side, they hurried away. Emily stared wide-eyed at the water in the harbor, at the tide flowing dark and swift, the ripples of the current curling silver into the deepening twilight. A green leaf swirled helplessly out with the tide, turning and twisting as it went.

In a daze, Emily made her way through town to the Little Harbor. She knew that she had to sail her boat out to the end of Marblehead Neck, but she could make no clear thoughts. If a tidal wave had suddenly swept Lucy out to sea, Emily could not have been more shocked and distressed. She took shortcuts and turnings by blind memory, hardly knowing where she was. In the shadow of a dry-docked boat, a wave of sickness surged up through her. Emily stopped to fight down the nausea. Then she moved on.

Tears ran unheeded down her face as she stumbled around a stack of lobster traps, and the Little Harbor opened before her. Its ragtag band of sundry small craft bobbed and strained against their painters in the receding tide. Everything was fleeing from her. With a sob, she ran out onto the dock.

"There you are!"

In panic, Emily spun around. Blount walked across the shingle of pebbles and broken shells toward her, his footsteps crunching loudly in the silence. Emily ducked her head and hastily wiped her face with her sleeve. In the press and urgency of the evening, she had forgotten that Blount was to meet her there. Her pulse galloped.

"I hope Moses was a help to you," Blount said, joining her on the dock.

"Yes." Emily's voice was rough. "Yes, he was, thank you."

Blount frowned. "What happened? You're very upset."

"No, no, I'm fine," Emily lied, frantically trying to judge how far Lucy and Moses could have gotten. They must still be in town, she guessed. The low causeway to the Neck and the rough paths among the rocks would take them more than half an hour to traverse, even if they ran.

With shaking hands, Emily began to work at the knots on the *Rosy's* lines. Blount stepped down into the boat and began to ready the sail.

"I'd like to think I know why you're so upset," Blount said in a quiet voice. He glanced up at her. "I can't believe I'm leaving tomorrow."

"No," Emily said, almost unable to control her voice. She looked away, pretending to study the wind. She felt as though a great roaring tempest were turning inside her, howling to get out. "Nor can I," she whispered.

For a moment, she had to close her eyes while she tried to master the emotions that assailed her from every side. Then, drawing an unsteady breath, she turned to face Blount.

"I'm sorry you have to go," she said truthfully. "And I will miss you."

Blount reached for her hand. "I'll write to you."

"You may not wish to," Emily told him, stepping down into the boat. She busied herself with the lines. "You may decide once you leave here that I'm not at all what you thought and that you don't wish to continue our friendship."

"That's impossible," he said fervently. "I could never think of you as anything but what you are: brave and sweet and honest."

"Please, don't," Emily said painfully. She looked down, and the breeze buffeted her so that she had to steady herself against the mast. She gripped it tightly. "Let's not talk that way or speak of parting. Let's only enjoy this last sail."

"If that's what you want."

"It is."

Filled with sadness, Emily turned and ran the sail up the mast. Almost immediately, the gusting breeze bellied out the sail, and the *Rosy* moved with surprising swiftness away from the dock. Emily was thankful for the busy concerns of getting under way, for it allowed her a space of time to gather her thoughts. She sat at the tiller, looping the mainsheet around her hand, and Blount leaned against the gunwale beside her, not speaking. The boat cut through the water with an almost soundless whisper in its wake, and Emily adjusted the tiller and line to make the most of the wind.

Then, almost fearfully, Emily looked over the starboard bow. Trelawney's ship had passed through the mouth of Marblehead Harbor. A jolt of fear punched through her.

"Look that way," she said, distracting Blount to the port side.

Blount followed her direction, turning away from the *Freedom*. "Yes?" he asked.

"Over there lies Dolliber's Cove," Emily stammered. "And Selman's Birth and Kettlebottom."

Beneath her hand, the tiller bucked as they hit the outgoing tide. Emily gripped it tighter and drew in on the sail. The *Rosy* heeled away from the wind, driving across the spate.

"I'll take the tiller," Blount offered. "The current looks strong."

"But I—" Emily looked at him uncertainly.

"You've taught me well," Blount assured her with a smile. "I'm sure I can manage."

Still, Emily hesitated. She did not know how much time she had to wait before making for the far side of the Neck. If she arrived too soon, Blount might well see Moses and Lucy scrambling along the rocky shore. If she arrived too late . . .

Blount sat beside her and put his hand over hers. Emily reluctantly lifted her eyes to his face.

"Don't you trust me?" Blount asked.

Her heart ached. The sky behind him was deepening into orange and pink, and his face was becoming shadowy and dim to her. Distantly she wondered if she would ever see him smile at her again, and guessed that she never would.

"Yes, I do," she said, relinquishing the tiller and mainsheet to him.

With a confident smile, Blount steered the craft out toward the end of Marblehead Neck. As they beat across the mouth of the harbor, the wind strengthened and the *Rosy* heeled over harder. The breeze rushed through Emily's hair, clawing through it like a witch's fingers. Ahead of them, the *Freedom* was a dark shape against the purple Atlantic horizon. Emily scanned the rocky promontory with anxious eyes.

"What do you suppose that ship is doing?" Blount asked, raising his voice against the rushing wind.

Emily shook her head, feigning deafness. Their wake

sprayed from the bow, and the wind cut across the top of the wave, showering them with drops of brine. Emily's eyes stung.

"You might almost imagine they're waiting for something," Blount shouted. "What could it be?"

Emily did not know what to say. Her mind was racing, and she could think of no sensible answer. She leaned forward, straining to see among the rocks through the failing light. The boat leaped over a wave with a smack. In that instant, Emily glimpsed Lucy and Moses as they slipped out of sight behind a boulder. Quickly Emily turned to see if Blount had spied them, but he was busy watching the sail. Emily leaned toward him.

"Let me bring the boat around the Neck, and we'll tie up. We can take a walk while there's still light."

Blount nodded, and his teeth gleamed whitely in the dimness. Emily took the tiller and sheet, and maneuvered the small boat toward the rocks. The waves foamed and surged among the boulders, dashing up and falling back. Emily watched carefully for the tiny bowl-shaped recess where she knew she could take in the *Rosy*. The wind gusted and rushed around them.

"There's an iron chain embedded in the rocks," Emily shouted to Blount. "When I come hard about, lean over the starboard gun'l and catch hold of it!"

He nodded. His eyes were wide with excitement as the boat slipped through the water toward the rocks. Emily's full concentration was fixed on the inlet, on the shifting winds and the waves. The opening was straight ahead.

166

She held her breath as the boat shot between two wave-washed rocks, and the rocky bulk of the Neck loomed above them. From the rocks ahead dangled a heavy rusted chain, dripping with seaweed. Emily let out the mainsheet and pushed the tiller hard around.

"Now!"

Blount leaned out over the starboard side and grabbed the chain, but as he did, the boat pitched on a wave and he lost his balance, falling halfway from the boat.

"No!" Emily lunged for him, and the boat, untended, swung around into the rock. The *Rosy* cracked sharply against the rocks, and Emily was thrown backward, dragging Blount with her.

"Oh, God," she cried, holding him tight for a moment.

Blount was panting with exertion and wet to the shoulders, but victoriously held aloft the slippery end of the chain. "I'd do it again to have you hold me this way," he said as Emily released him.

The wind whistled over the tops of the rocks and did not reach them in the shelter of the tiny recess, but the boat was rocked up and down by the waves that sucked in and out through the narrow gap.

"Are you hurt?" Emily asked, feeling the blood slow in her veins.

"No, I'm not," Blount said. "But I'll be glad to be on dry land for a few minutes."

Emily and Blount made the *Rosy* fast to the chain as

the hull ground and thumped against the rocks. Emily cringed at the sound.

"Will the boat be safe?" Blount asked.

"Yes." Emily knew that Lucy and Moses would take it off the rocks before it sustained too much damage, but she prayed that they would be quick. "Come on."

She hitched up her skirts in one hand, jumped out onto a rock, and scrambled breathlessly upwards, Blount climbing at her side and helping her in the steep places. As they reached the top, the wide sweep of the Atlantic opened up before them. A quarter of a mile away, the *Freedom* was waiting.

"You're trembling," Blount said, taking Emily's hand.

"I—I was frightened for you," she said. "I thought you would be thrown on the rocks."

Blount brushed away a lock of hair that kept blowing across Emily's face. He was shivering.

"Let's get out of the wind," he said, leading her away from the rocky summit.

Emily cast one anxious glance over her shoulder as they walked over the short, springy turf between the rocks. Then she saw Lucy and Moses begin to descend to the *Rosy*. She faced forward again, suddenly blinded with tears.

"I'm going to talk to my parents," Blount was saying. "I have been attending the University of Virginia, but I'm going to change to Harvard. That won't be any distance at all from here."

"No," Emily whispered. She stumbled, and Blount caught her in his arms.

"Emily, what, you're crying," Blount exclaimed. "Oh, sweetheart."

"Blount, no, you don't understand," Emily cried.

Overcome with guilt and grief, she broke away from him and ran up onto a rock. Through her tears she saw her sailboat, with Lucy at the tiller and Moses in the bow, plying across the choppy waves toward the *Freedom* in the failing light. Lucy looked back and lifted one hand in farewell.

Emily clenched her fists at her sides to keep from shaking. She heard the scrape of Blount's boots on the rock behind her.

"Emily, I can't bear to see you so upset," Blount said, taking her hand.

She could not speak. Frowning, he followed her gaze.

"Your boat," he exclaimed.

When Emily still did not speak, he squinted hard to see the figures in the *Rosy*. He was utterly silent, and because of that Emily knew that he understood at last the cause of her grief. Her heart full, Emily looked up at him.

"I'm sorry," she whispered.

Blount's nostrils were pinched, and there were tears in the corners of his eyes. He looked at her with pain and bewilderment in his face. "But, Emily, I loved you."

"I know," Emily said. Tears spilled down her cheeks as she put one hand on his heart. "I wanted to love you, too."

He pressed her hand hard against him, and then

turned abruptly away, stumbling among the rocks. Emily looked out to sea again. The *Freedom* was laying on sail and already moving, and drifting away from it on the dark water was the empty *Rosy*. As Emily's legs folded beneath her, she collapsed on the ground and buried her face in her hands.

When Emily trudged back into town later, it was dark, and light spilled from windows onto the streets. She raised her head to look into one window and saw an old couple sitting at a table, playing piquet by candlelight. As she watched, the man flung down a discard with a dramatic flourish, and his wife patted his hand, smiling indulgently.

Emily bent her head and went on to the Wild Rose. Cheerful voices reached her on the street from inside the tavern. She passed by the front door and went through the garden gate and into the kitchen.

Lavinia, seated at the table, looked up with shining eyes. "Oh, Em!" she exclaimed, holding up a letter. "A sailor just walked over from Salem to bring me this. It's from Zachary, and he's well. He's very well! And they aim to be back by October. Listen to what he says," she went on, holding the letter to the light.

As Lavinia breathlessly read through her husband's letter, Emily sank into a chair. Her sister's voice faded to a distant hum in her ears, and the golden lamplight seemed to shine brighter and brighter as Emily's eyes filled again with tears. On the table beside the lamp was Lucy's well-worn copy of McGuffey's *Eclectic Reader*.

"Lavvy," Emily whispered.

Lavinia faltered to a stop, and looked up at Emily with an inquisitive, happy smile. "Yes, what is it, Em?"

Emily swallowed with difficulty. "Lucy's gone, Lavvy. She ran away with Moses and we'll never see her again."

"What?" Lavinia lowered Zachary's letter to her lap. "What happened?"

"I arranged for Moses to run away, and Lucy went with him." Emily choked. "She told me to give you and Father her love."

Lavinia came around to Emily's side and put her arms around her. "Oh, my dear." They put their heads on one another's shoulders.

A commotion at the front of the house gradually asserted itself in the kitchen. Emily and Lavinia looked toward the door as they heard the tread of many footsteps. The door opened, and Mr. MacKenzie entered, followed by Mr. Stockwell, Blount, Mr. Pinkham, and several onlookers from the tavern.

Emily rose from her chair and stood next to Lavinia, her back to the table. She could not bring herself to look at Blount.

"I'm going to get to the bottom of this," Mr. Stockwell said threateningly. "Miss MacKenzie, what role did you have in this crime?"

"Crime?" Emily repeated. Her mind was blank. She knew Blount was looking at her, and she could not bear to see the hurt in his eyes. She groped for Lavinia's hand. Lavinia returned her pressure.

"As I told you," Mr. MacKenzie said. "My younger daughter is just a girl and can have had nothing to do with this."

"That's not what I think," Mr. Pinkham said. "I saw her conspiring with them."

Mr. Stockwell glared at Emily's father. "If I find that she did have a hand in stealing Moses, I will sue you for every dollar you have and bring this house down around your heads." He rounded on Emily. "Now, my son tells me you and he went sailing and that Moses and your nigger girl took the boat."

"Yes," Emily said gruffly. She cleared her throat to speak louder. "Yes, that is what happened."

"Just the way you planned it, no doubt," Mr. Stockwell shouted furiously.

"Father—" Blount stepped forward. "From what I saw, Moses and the girl were out there courting, and they saw the opportunity to steal the boat."

"Them niggers is sneaky, every one of them," Mr. Pinkham sneered. "And they'll thieve a thing as soon as look at it."

Mr. MacKenzie gave the bounty hunter a look of loathing. "Get out of my house."

"But the law—"

"Get out. I won't have anyone speak of my daughter Lucy in this way. I won't have anyone say *nigger* under this roof."

With a dry laugh, Mr. Pinkham ran his finger under his collar and shrugged. "I guess I'll wait outside."

Mr. Stockwell looked on thunderously as the bounty hunter ambled through the back door. Then he rounded on Emily's father. "What is your answer, sir?"

"Mister, if your son says this is what happened, I have no doubt that that is what happened."

"And if it weren't," Lavinia added dryly, "I assure you that Emily would never admit it."

Red with anger, Mr. Stockwell jabbed Blount in the chest with one finger. "So help me, boy, if you're lying to me, you'll regret it."

"Father, I give you my word as a gentleman," Blount said, sending Emily a quick glance.

She raised her chin and waited. If he chose to tell the truth, she could not blame him. He must think she had led him on falsely from the start, and then deliberately tried to kill him.

Blount looked squarely at his father. "I invited Miss MacKenzie to take me sailing this evening. I think she could hardly have plotted to steal our slave from under my nose. I repeat, I invited her."

"You did, did you?" Mr. Stockwell blustered.

"I think we must assume that Moses and Lucy were the agents of their own escape," Mr. MacKenzie said. "And as there are no charges to press and no lawsuit to pursue, I suggest that you cut your losses."

"Good advice," piped up Mr. Ledue from the hall-way.

"I will, and all of you be damned," Mr. Stockwell

said, giving the assembled group a dark, hate-filled look. "You'll find meddling in other folks' business is bad business, however."

He turned and stormed out. Blount looked sorrowfully at Emily, and then quietly followed his father.

"There, that's the end of that," Mr. MacKenzie said to the crowd in the passageway. "Go on to the front of the house and I'll stand you all a round of drinks."

There was a boisterous murmuring and babble of talk as the crowd retreated. Mr. MacKenzie turned back from the doorway and looked at Emily. Coal settled in the stove, and the lamp flared briefly, sending up a thin banner of smoke.

"Your mother would be proud, Em," Mr. MacKenzie said quietly.

He turned and left the kitchen. Lavinia put her arm around Emily's waist, and Emily rested her head against her sister's shoulder.

"Oh, Lavinia, I'm so tired."

"I know, dear," Lavinia murmured, gently stroking Emily's cheek. "I'm tired, too."

Emily left the kitchen and trudged up the stairs to her room. Her legs were shaking as she closed the door behind her, and she sank to her knees beside the bed. For thirteen years she had rested her head beside Lucy's, and shared her secrets and her sorrows. She could not believe her sister was gone so suddenly. It did not seem possible.

Slowly, Emily lifted her head, and saw an envelope on the pillow. It was addressed to her in Lucy's strong, slanting script. Emily slipped the single sheet from the envelope and sat on the bed to read.

*Dearest Emily—*

*I'm not leaving you. You must believe that. I'll always be with you and Lavvy and Uncle Marcus. I'm part of the Wild Rose and always will be, and I only hope I can come home one day. You must believe me: it is my fondest hope. I entrust you with the task of making it bearable for me to return and possible for Moses to come home with me.*

*Until that day I remain your loving sister,*

*Lucy*

Emily awoke later than usual the next morning. When she opened her eyes, the sun's path had traveled halfway across the bedroom. Blinking sleepily, Emily went to the window to look at the day.

The sun was dazzling, and a sweet, fresh breeze brought the sounds of traffic and voices, dogs and laughter. Two girls walked arm in arm down the street below her, giggling and whispering to one another, their gingham dresses as bright as flowers. Emily felt remote from them and from the busy noises around her; she felt as though she'd been wrapped up in winter woolens, and was muffled from touch and sensation.

But as she gazed out toward the dazzling brightness that hovered over the harbor and the ocean beyond, she felt a glimmer of bittersweet gladness. It was a fine day for sailing. The *Freedom* must be well on its way to Canada, cutting through the water like a dolphin.

Emily felt a strong desire to put her hands in the water, to let it draw the heat from her blood. The more she considered it, the stronger the impulse became. She dressed hastily, and slipped out of the house and hurried to the Little Harbor. If she could put her hands in the water, she would have one last connection to Lucy, as though her friend could feel her touch across the waves.

But as Emily reached the boatyard, her footsteps slowed. She knew she would see only an empty spot at the dock where her boat had always been tied. Slowly she turned the corner and faced the harbor.

Micah was standing in his sailboat at the dock, readying her for a sail. Emily stepped backward involuntarily, knocking over an oar that had been propped against a shed. It fell to the ground with a wooden clunk. Micah glanced up, shielding his eyes against the glare off the water. She saw the white flash of his teeth in his tanned face.

Wiping his hands on his britches, Micah sprang out of the boat onto the dock, and came toward Emily. She shrank back.

"Emily, I wanted to tell you," he began. "I'm sorry about Lucy. I know you'll miss her."

Emily looked down at the ground and nodded.

He squinted out at the water. "Those folks from Virginia left first thing." Micah looked back at her and suddenly frowned. "Did you care for him, honestly?"

Emily was tempted to tell him it was none of his

business, but she did not have the heart for it. She sighed and shook her head. "I thought I did," she admitted. "I wanted to. And I tried to overlook the fact that he lives with slavery. But in the end . . ."

"In the end you discovered you have a conscience," Micah said with a sly grin.

Emily moved away from him. "Well, I admit it might not be such a highly developed organ yet as you no doubt have," she said sarcastically.

"Oh, you'd be surprised what a conscience I've got." Micah laughed.

"Surprise me," Emily said. "I'd like to see a Handy with a conscience."

He leaned against the wall of the shed and looked at her in silence for a moment. "You know, Emily, I'm tempted to think that you might actually like me if I had a different name. But to accuse you of having an irrational bias against someone over a paltry thing like family . . ."

"Are you saying I have an irrational bias against you?" Emily asked through gritted teeth.

"Yes, I am," Micah said. "And to show you how irrational and unfounded it is, I'm going to surprise you by doing you a good turn."

Emily shook her head. "Please don't go to any trouble on my account."

But Micah leaned forward to take her hand. "Come on," he said, pulling her toward the dock. "Let's go see if we can't find your boat."

In spite of herself, Emily felt her heart leap with hope. "Do you think we could?" she asked.

177

Micah jumped down into his boat and handed her in after him. He gave her a grin and shrugged. "We can look, can't we? Who knows, once we start looking, we might find something unexpected."

Emily settled herself in the bow and folded her arms around her knees. She frowned thoughtfully at Micah as he readied the sail. "I refuse to think well of you, you know."

Micah laughed as he cast off, and the boat sprang forward. With a smile, Emily shook the hair from her eyes and turned to meet the Atlantic.

Follow the sweeping saga of generations
of young MacKenzie women growing up
at the Wild Rose Inn.

## LAURA OF THE WILD ROSE INN
## 1898

*On the eve of the twentieth century, the world is chang-*
*ing rapidly, and sixteen-year-old Laura MacKenzie*
*wants to be a part of the coming age. Her parents,*
*forever entrenched in their old-fashioned ways, are*
*running the Wild Rose Inn the same way their family*
*has for two centuries. Laura is sure there must be more*
*to life than she finds in rustic Marblehead, Massachu-*
*setts, if only she were given the chance to leave and*
*seek her destiny for herself.*

*When Laura meets Grant Van Doren, a student at*
*Yale, she's introduced to new possibilities. Laura can*
*almost taste the freedom and adventures Grant and the*
*new era offer her. Under Grant's spell, all seems possi-*
*ble. Can Laura depend on Grant and his promises, or*
*is her future something she must find for herself?*

## CLAIRE OF THE WILD ROSE INN
## 1928

*Since her father's death, Claire MacKenzie has kept afloat the Wild Rose Inn, her family's business for generations. But now that Prohibition has made serving liquor illegal, the Wild Rose cannot compete with the speakeasies that peddle bootleg alcohol. Claire's brother, Bob, wants to make the Wild Rose profitable by turning it into a speakeasy, but Claire doesn't want to be involved in anything criminal.*

*Then Claire finds the town drunk shot dead on his boat. Police Chief Handy dismisses the case, but Claire wants answers. Her only ally is Hank Logan, a reporter looking for a scoop. Together they investigate, and every lead brings Claire closer to Hank—and closer to trouble at home. Will Claire risk her family, the Wild Rose Inn, and her new love for Hank to get to the dangerous truth?*

## GRACE OF THE WILD ROSE INN
## 1944

*Grace MacKenzie has been achingly lonely since her brother, Mark, and her fiancé, Jimmy Penworthy, have both been sent to the European front. Yet, working hard on the homefront for the war effort, Grace has gained a sense of independence and inner strength.*

*When the boys finally come home, Grace is heart-broken at how the war has changed her fiancé. A wounded war hero in the eyes of the town, he brags about his experiences while stubbornly insisting that Grace give up her dream to continue to run the Wild Rose Inn after they marry. Grace is confused by her changed feelings for Jimmy—she's angry that he doesn't understand her ambition and yet she feels guilty that she's not the girl Jimmy remembers and still wants her to be.*

*But Jimmy hasn't returned home alone—his army buddy Mike is everything she'd hoped to find in Jimmy. Where will Grace's heart lead her as she must decide her future, the future of those who love her, and the fate of her family's Wild Rose Inn?*

## ABOUT THE AUTHOR

Jennifer Armstrong is the author of many books for children and young adults, including the historical novel *Steal Away,* the Pets, Inc. series, and several picture books.

Jennifer Armstrong lives in Saratoga Springs, New York, in a house more than 150 years old that is reputed to have been a tavern. In addition to writing, she raises guide-dog puppies and works in her garden, where roses grow around the garden gate.